Claudia was pregnant.

Placing a hand on her still-flat belly, she closed her eyes and breathed in slowly. Now that the shock and pain of Ciro's betrayal had dimmed to a dull ache, her path was clear, and real unfettered freedom beckoned.

After two weeks spent thinking and planning and channeling her heroines, she knew what she had to do.

She had to leave Sicily. Whatever happened, she would not raise her child here. Her father's reach was too great. She would be at his mercy—and so would her child.

She would never be again.

And nor would she go running to her sister, Imma, not unless worse came to worst and it became absolutely necessary. She prayed for her child's sake that it didn't. She prayed that she could build a cordiality with her enemy.

Just reaching for her phone set her heart off at a canter. She spoke into it. "Unblock Ciro." Like magic, her phone unblocked him. She spoke into it again. "Call Ciro."

She only had to wait two rings before he answered. "Claudia?"

Michelle Smart's love affair with books started when she was a baby, when she would cuddle them in her cot. A voracious reader of all genres, she found her love of romance established when she stumbled across her first Harlequin book at the age of twelve. She's been reading—and writing—them ever since. Michelle lives in Northamptonshire, England, with her husband and two young Smarties.

Books by Michelle Smart

Harlequin Presents

Her Greek Wedding Night Debt

Conveniently Wed!

The Sicilian's Bought Cinderella

Cinderella Seductions

A Cinderella to Secure His Heir
The Greek's Pregnant Cinderella

Passion in Paradise

A Passionate Reunion in Fiji

Rings of Vengeance

Billionaire's Bride for Revenge
Marriage Made in Blackmail
Billionaire's Baby of Redemption

Visit the Author Profile page
at Harlequin.com for more titles.

Michelle Smart

—

A BABY TO BIND
HIS INNOCENT

HARLEQUIN
PRESENTS

Recycling programs for this product may not exist in your area.

ISBN-13: 978-1-335-89381-9

A Baby to Bind His Innocent

Copyright © 2020 by Michelle Smart

This edition published by arrangement with Harlequin Books S.A.

For questions and comments about the quality of this book, please contact us at CustomerService@Harlequin.com.

Harlequin Enterprises ULC
22 Adelaide St. West, 40th Floor
Toronto, Ontario M5H 4E3, Canada
www.Harlequin.com

Printed in U.S.A.

A BABY TO BIND
HIS INNOCENT

This book is for my partner in crime, Louise Fuller.
Thank you for making Ciro and Claudia's book
such a joy to write. xxx

PROLOGUE

'WE MUST FIX THIS.' Ciro Trapani drained his bourbon and fixed his eyes on his brother's shattered face.

The past four days had seen Vicenzu age by a decade. The ready smile had been lost, and the always amused eyes were now dank, murky pools of grief. And guilt.

They both shared the grief and guilt, but for Vicenzu the guilt was double.

After a long pause, in which Vicenzu drained his own drink, he finally met Ciro's stare. His features twisted and he gave a sharp nod.

'We have to get it back,' Ciro stated. 'All of it.'

Another nod.

Ciro leaned forward. He needed to be certain that whatever they agreed today, Vicenzu would stick to it.

The family business was gone. Stolen.

The family home was gone. Stolen.

Their father was dead.

Ciro had looked up to his brother his entire life and, while their personalities and temperaments differed, they'd always been close. The man sharing a table with him in this Palermo bar was a stranger. He knew Vicenzu thought they should wait for a decent mourning period to pass before they did anything to avenge their father but the fury in Ciro needed to put plans into action *now*. And Vicenzu needed to play his part. What had been stolen would be recovered by whatever means necessary. Their devastated mother needed her home back.

'Vicenzu?'

His brother slumped in his chair and closed his eyes. After another long pause, he finally spoke. 'Yes, I know what I have to do, and I'll do it. I will take the business back.'

Ciro pressed his lips together and narrowed his eyes. Cesare Buscetta, their father's childhood tormentor, the thief who'd legally stolen their parents' business and home, had gifted the business to his oldest daughter, the inappropriately named Immacolata. Right then, Ciro did not believe Vicenzu had the wits about him to take her on and win. Vicenzu had always been closer to their father than Ciro. His sudden death four days ago and the subsequent revelations of everything that had been stolen had all contributed to mute his brother's natural exuberance and turn him into this lost ghost-like person.

Vicenzu must have recognised the cynicism in his brother's expression for he straightened. 'I will get the business back, Ciro. This is my responsibility. Mine.'

'You are sure you can handle it?' A question he would never have needed to pose four days ago before their world had been ripped apart. Getting the family home back would be a much easier task. Cesare had gifted the house to his younger daughter. From what Ciro had gleaned about the reclusive Claudia Buscetta, she was a spoilt, pampered princess with a brain that compared unfavourably to a rocking horse.

His brother's nostrils flared, a glimmer of the old spark flashing from his eyes. 'Yes. You get the house back for Mamma and leave the business to me.'

Ciro contemplated him a little longer before inclining his head. 'As you wish.' He caught a passing bartender's eye and indicated another round of drinks for them before addressing his brother again. 'You must stop blaming yourself. You weren't to know. Papà should have confided in us.' That he hadn't was something they would both have to live with.

'If I hadn't borrowed all that money from him he would never have been forced to sell.'

'If I'd made more visits home I would have been on hand to help,' Ciro countered grimly. This was the guilt that lay so heavily in him. He hadn't been home to Sicily since Christmas. The sabotage against his father had started in the new year. 'Papà should have told you—told both of us—how precarious the family finances were but what's done is done. The only person to blame is that bastard Cesare. And his daughters,' he added, his top lip curling with distaste.

Fresh drinks were placed before them. Ciro raised his glass aloft. 'To vengeance.'

'To vengeance,' Vicenzu echoed.

They clinked their glasses and knocked back the fiery liquid.

The plan was sealed.

CHAPTER ONE

One week later

CLAUDIA BUSCETTA WIPED the copper worktop clean, listening hard to the romantic story being narrated on her audio device, her heart so full she didn't know how to contain it.

She'd only lived under this roof for ten days but already it felt like home. This was no ostentatious show home like the sprawling villa she'd grown up in. This was a true home, with a wonderfully equipped kitchen in which she could bake to her heart's content, and a vegetable garden and orchard large enough for her to grow all the fruit and vegetables she could manage.

For the first time in her twenty-one years, Claudia was all alone...unless she counted the security guards her father had posted outside the grounds. He'd wanted to have them housed inside with her but mercifully her older sister, Immacolata, had made him see reason. After all, the business Imma had been gifted adjoined the farmhouse and its estate that their father had bestowed on Claudia. Imma would be on hand to help if Claudia got into any difficulty, just as she'd always been there to help throughout her life.

Of course, her father had made her promise never to leave her new home alone. She must always be accompanied by two bodyguards. As if she could go anywhere without them! She couldn't drive. The nearest village was a mile away on top of the hill filled with the olive groves that constituted the main part of Imma's new business but there were no shops there. If Claudia wanted to go shopping she needed to be driven.

A loud buzz rang out, startling her. Pausing the audiobook, she pressed the intercom her father had installed on the kitchen wall. 'Hello?'

One of the security guards spoke. 'There is a Ciro Trapani here to see you.'

'Who?'

'Ciro Trapani.'

The name meant nothing to her. 'What does he want?'

'He says it's a private matter.'

'My father has approved this?' She supposed he must have done if the security guards were prepared to give her the choice of letting this

Ciro man into her new sanctuary. Claudia's approval was only required after her father had given his. That was the way of her world.

'Yes.'

'Okay. Let him in.'

Curious, she opened the front door and stood outside to wait. A sleek black car drove slowly towards her. She caught the tail-end of the electric gates closing in the distance.

The car came to a stop in front of the triple garage to the side of the farmhouse. Strange. Her visitors so far, which had consisted of her father, her sister and the family lawyer, had all parked at the front of the house.

Her curiosity evaporated when the driver unfolded himself out of the car and she found herself staring at the sexiest man to have ever graced her eyes. Impossibly tall, with thick dark hair in a quiff and oozing vitality, he could have walked off the cover of a men's health magazine.

He sauntered towards her with an easy laconic stroll and an even easier laconic smile on a face hidden beneath aviator shades.

Noting the hand-stitched dark grey suit he wore over an open-necked pale blue shirt and polished black brogues, Claudia surreptitiously dusted off the flour still clinging to her long black cotton top and silently kicked herself for not changing out of her jeans, which had grass stains at the knees from her early-morning bout of weeding.

When he reached her, he pulled the shades off and fixed her with a dimpled smile that would make a nun's knees go weak. Fitting, seeing as it made *her* knees go weak and she'd once seriously contemplated joining a convent.

'Miss Buscetta?' Green eyes sparkled. A large hand with a glimpse of fine dark hair at his wrist extended towards her.

That *voice*. Oh, it was rich and deep and it made her toes grind into her slippers.

A crease appeared in his handsome brow and, with horror, she realised she'd been too busy gawping at him to either reply or take his offered hand.

But was it any wonder? She'd never met a man like this before. The only men outside her family she was acquainted with were her father's employees.

Pulling herself together, she clasped the long, tapered fingers with her own and felt a surge of warmth flow through her veins. Unsettled, she quickly released them.

'I'm Ciro Trapani. Forgive me for turning up like this but I was in the neighbourhood. Would you mind very much if I were to say goodbye to this place?'

Now Claudia's brow was the one to crease.

Say goodbye? What on earth was he talking about?

He flashed his dimpled grin at her again. 'This estate belonged to my parents. I grew up in this house. They sold it to your father before I had a chance to say goodbye to it.'

'You lived here?' Claudia knew nothing about the previous owners other than their obvious love for their home.

'For the first eighteen years of my life, yes. I live in America now but this has always been home to me. My only regret is that I never came back to Sicily in time to say goodbye before the deeds were transferred.'

Oh, the poor man. How sad for him. Claudia would always make regular visits to the villa she'd been raised in so had had no need to say goodbye.

He must have taken her silence for a refusal for he raised his broad shoulders and shook his head ruefully. 'I'm sorry. I'm a stranger to you. I was being sentimental. I'll leave you to get on with your day.'

When he turned his back and took a step away, she realised he was going to leave. 'You can come in.'

He looked back at her, a quizzical expression on his handsome face. 'I don't want to impose.'

She laced her fingers together. 'You're not imposing.'

'You're sure?'

'Definitely.' She swept an arm towards the door. 'Please, come in.'

Ciro followed her inside, hiding his smirk of satisfaction at how easily he'd made it through the doors. A week of careful preparation and things were going exactly to plan.

'Can I make you a coffee?' she asked as she led him to the kitchen.

'That would be great, thank you. Something smells good.'

She blushed. 'I've been baking. Please, take a seat.'

While she busied herself with the coffee machine, Ciro sat himself at a kitchen table that should never have been placed there and took the opportunity to study her. He must not allow himself to take too much notice of all the new kitchen furnishings or the fury he had under tight control would explode from him and his thirst for revenge would be over before it began.

He'd been all for coming straight to the house after he'd made his pact with Vicenzu. Patience had never been one of his strengths but he'd had enough awareness to know he couldn't meet Claudia Buscetta until he had his emotions under a better degree of control.

She was much prettier than he'd envisaged. Chestnut hair with subtle gold highlights was tied in a loose plait that fell halfway down her back and framed a beguiling face with huge dark brown eyes, pretty rounded cheekbones, a snub nose and generous lips. Shorter than he'd envisaged too, she looked slender beneath the shapeless oversized top she wore. That she had a wholesome air of innocence he considered laughable but her attractiveness was welcome. It would make his seduction more palatable.

'Where in America do you live?' she asked as she opened a cupboard and removed two mugs from it. This particular cupboard had, until less than two weeks ago, contained an abundance of dried pasta. The shelf beside it that had housed his mother's recipe books now had colourful ornaments on it.

'New York.'

'Isn't New York dangerous?'

'No more dangerous than any other major city.'

Her perplexed eyes met his briefly. 'Oh. I thought…' She blinked, shook her head and opened the fridge. 'How do you take your coffee?'

'Black, no sugar.'

The oven's timer went off. It was such a familiar sound that Ciro clenched his hands into fists to stop fresh rage bursting out. His childhood had been punctuated with that timer beeping, always followed moments later by his mother's call for dinner.

Protecting her hands with oven gloves, Claudia removed the item, filling the kitchen with even more of that evocative pastry scent. By the time she'd finished, the coffee was ready. She brought the mugs to the table and sat across from him. When she met his eye he was intrigued to see a flush cover her cheeks before she darted her gaze away.

'How are you settling in?' he asked.

'Very well.' She jumped back to her feet. 'Biscuit?'

'Sure.'

She returned with a ceramic tub and removed the lid. 'I made these yesterday so they should still be fresh.'

He helped himself and took a bite. Immediately, his mouth filled with heaven. 'These are amazing.'

The same flush of pleasure as when he'd complimented the smell that had filled the kitchen covered her face again. 'Thank you… Would you like some of the apricot tart when it's cooled down? If you're still here…' More colour stained her face. 'I'm sure you have things to be getting on with.'

'Actually, I don't.' He took a sip of his coffee and eyed her openly. 'I'm on a short vacation.'

'Oh?'

'My father died recently. I'm trying to sort his affairs and help my mother.'

Her next, 'Oh,' had a very different inflection. 'I'm sorry. That's awful. I didn't know.'

Sure you didn't, he thought cynically. *He only died the day after your father legally stole this house for you.*

'He had a heart attack.'

She was an excellent actress for her large, soft brown eyes brimmed with sympathy. 'I'm sorry,' she repeated. 'I can't begin to imagine how you're feeling.'

'Like I've been shot in the heart. He was only sixty.'

'That's no age.'

'No age at all. We assumed he had decades left.' He gave a theatrical shake of his head. Claudia Buscetta might be an excellent actress but she had nothing on Ciro, who'd had a week to prepare for this moment and knew exactly how he was going to orchestrate things. 'It's the regrets that play on the mind. If I ever marry and have children—which I really hope to do if I ever fall in love—he won't meet them. My children will grow up not knowing their grand-

father. If I'd known the stress he was under...'
He gave another shake of his head.

'Is that what caused it? Stress?'

'We think so. My parents have had a lot to deal with recently.'

A very pretty hand fluttered to her mouth. 'It wasn't connected with them moving from the house, was it?'

Having the house stolen from them, I think you mean.

'It was an accumulation of things.'

'I can see how much your parents loved this house.' She cradled her mug with both hands. 'I know they felt it necessary to downsize but it must have been difficult for them.'

How she uttered that complete rubbish with a straight face beggared belief. But then, she was a Buscetta, a family which straddled the line between legal and illegal like a circus of tightrope walkers. Ciro's father, Alessandro, had gone to school with Cesare. Even as a child Cesare had been a thug who'd terrorised everyone, including the teachers. Ciro had only met Cesare for the first time that day but his name had been synonymous with thuggery and criminality in the Trapani house for as far back as Ciro could remember.

He supposed Claudia had adopted the downsizing line as a way to salve her conscience. It had to be easier to sleep at night than admit the truth that her father had bribed a senior member of Alessandro Trapani's staff to sabotage the business until he was on his knees financially and had no choice but to sell both the family home he'd planned to grow old in with his beloved wife and the business that had been in the Trapani family for generations.

Instead of unleashing the vitriol burning the back of his throat, Ciro kept his focus on the long-term objective and folded his arms on the table while he stared at her. 'It was difficult. What makes it worse is that I wasn't here for them. I should have been. That's what sons do. They take care of their parents and shoulder their burdens. It's something I'll always have to live with but, for now, I have to look after my *mamma.*'

'How is she coping?' she asked softly.

He grimaced. 'Not great. She's staying with her sister in Florence and taking things one day at a time but I'm hoping she'll be ready to move back to Sicily soon.' *Once I've taken this house back for her.* 'I'm sorry. I didn't mean to depress you.'

'Don't apologise.'

'I don't know why I just told you all that. I don't even know you.' He made sure the look in his eyes told her how much he would like to get to know her.

The pink staining her cheeks told him she understood the silent message. Not only that she understood it but that she was receptive to it. Ciro, while not being a playboy of his brother's standard, had never had a shortage of women willing to throw themselves at him. It was amazing what billionaire status coupled with looks the world considered handsome did for a man's sex appeal. As such, he was something of an expert at reading a woman's body language and the language he was reading from Miss Buscetta was one of interest.

He'd spent the past week learning as much as he could about her. He'd been disappointed to find there wasn't much to learn. Educated in a convent until she was sixteen, she had, until only ten days ago, lived the life of a recluse in her father's heavily guarded villa. He would bet his last cent that she was a virgin; a rosebud waiting for a man to set her into bloom. Only a man with immense wealth and a scandal-free history would be allowed to touch one of Cesare Buscetta's precious daughters. A man such as Ciro himself.

A man like Cesare Buscetta saw nothing wrong with the games he'd played to wrench the Trapani family home and business from them. To him, it was just business. Ciro knew this because he'd done more than just investigate Claudia's boring background. Before coming here he'd visited her father on the pretext of proposing a potential business deal. He'd held his nose and broken bread with his enemy because he'd needed to know how best to play the man's daughter. If Cesare had treated him with suspicion he would've engineered a meet with Claudia somewhere else. But Cesare, so arrogant in the justifications of his own actions, had welcomed Ciro like a long-lost son. He'd even had the nerve to mention the school days he'd shared with Alessandro. To hear Cesare speak of it, those days had been full of high japes and escapades. He'd failed to mention his penchant for flushing the heads of the kids who refused to pay protection money to him down the toilet, or the time he'd threatened Alessandro with a knife if he didn't complete a homework assignment for him.

When, at the end of their meeting, Ciro had casually mentioned he would like to pay a visit to his childhood home for one last sentimental goodbye, Cesare had immediately called the guards posted at the farmhouse to inform them that Ciro must be allowed entry if Claudia permitted it.

His lack of self-awareness was as breathtaking as his daughter's faux sympathy.

Ciro lifted his cheeks into a smile at the woman who was as much his enemy as her father. 'Ready to show me around?'

'You know the place better than I do. I don't mind if you want to say goodbye on your own.'

He shook his head slowly, making sure his eyes contained the right mix of interest in her and dolefulness at his situation. 'I can think of nothing I would like more than for you to accompany me...but only if you want to.'

She fingered the end of her plait, then gave a tiny nod.

Walking through his childhood home with Claudia Buscetta by his side, her body language telling him loud and clear that she was attracted to him, Ciro suppressed the laughter that wanted to break free.

This was going to be even easier than he'd thought. It was almost anticlimactic how perfectly it was all falling into his lap.

'You seem distracted, Princess.'

Claudia, who'd been daydreaming about a certain hunk of a man, looked at her father's bemused face and felt a blush burn her cheeks. They were sitting in the smaller of the villa's dining rooms at a table that could only seat twelve, her father at his customary place at the head, Claudia to his left. Dish upon dish of delicious delicacies had been brought out for them to share but she'd hardly noticed what she'd forked into her mouth. She felt as if she'd been floating ever since Ciro had left her home.

'I had a visitor today,' she confessed, knowing she wasn't telling him anything he didn't already know.

'Ciro Trapani?'

'Papà…' She tried not to cringe as she made her revelation. 'He's asked me on a date.'

Her father's beady eyes gleamed. 'And what did you say?'

'That I would think about it. But really, I wanted to ask you first.'

'Good girl.' He nodded his approval. 'And what answer do you want to give him?'

She closed her eyes then blurted it out. 'I want to say yes.'

'Then say yes.'

'Really?' She didn't dare expel a sigh of relief. Not yet. Her father took overprotectiveness to unimaginable heights. That Claudia was an adult had not changed this. Unlike her highly educated, clever sister who could, if she ever felt it necessary, break away from him and be self-sufficient, Claudia could not. She was dependent on him for everything. He'd gifted her a home but if she wanted the funds to maintain it and clothe herself, she needed to be as obedient as she'd always been, hence why she was at his dining table sharing a meal with him rather than eating dinner in her own home. He'd called not long after Ciro had left, inviting her over. Refusal had not been an option.

She loved her father…but she feared him too. Sometimes she hated him. The yearning for freedom and independence had been growing in intensity since adolescence, but she could never act upon it. She had never rebelled and never said no to him. She'd never dared. 'You don't mind?'

'He's a hardworking businessman from a good family—apart from his brother, that is—and with a good reputation. He's very rich, did you know that? Worth billions. And he's at the age when a man wants to settle down and find a wife.'

'*Papà!*' She felt her cheeks go crimson again.

Her father poured himself more wine. 'Why would he not consider you for a wife? You have impeccable pedigree. You're from a good, wealthy Sicilian family and you're as beautiful as your mother was.'

Claudia refused to show any of her distaste at this supposedly flattering assessment of her attributes, especially when her father so clearly admired Ciro enough that he had no objection to him taking his youngest daughter out.

'It's only a date,' she reminded him quietly. Her first ever date.

'My marriage to your mother started with a date. Her brothers came as chaperones.' He raised his glass to her. 'Go on your date but remember who you are and where you come from and the values I've instilled in you. They're values a man like Ciro Trapani will appreciate.' He downed his wine in one large swallow.

CHAPTER TWO

CLAUDIA SAT CONTENTEDLY at her childhood dressing table while her sister plaited her hair. It was something Imma had done for her hundreds of times throughout her life but never on a day like today. Claudia's wedding day. Their father had wanted to fly a famous hairdresser over from Milan to do her hair but on this, Claudia had got her own way. She wanted her big sister to do it.

'Any nerves?' Imma asked as she wound the thick plaits together, cleverly binding them with diamond pins that should—if all the practice they'd put into it worked—sparkle when the sun or any form of light fell upon them.

Claudia met her sister's stare in the mirror. 'Should I have?'

'I don't know.' Imma smiled. 'I've never been in love. I just wondered…you two have only known each other such a short time.'

'I've known him for two months.'

'Exactly!'

'What's the point in waiting when we both know what we feel is true?' Claudia said simply. 'I want to spend my life with him. Nothing will change that.'

She'd known by the end of their first date that she was half in love with Ciro. He made her feel giddy, as if she could dance on air. For the first time too, she'd sensed an escape route from her life. He'd proposed two weeks later, having already asked her father's permission. The speed of the proposal had taken her aback but she hadn't hesitated to say yes.

Until Ciro had come into her life, she'd been trapped. Her life had had no meaning and no means of getting any. What kind of employment could a woman unable to read or write and who struggled with numbers get? Claudia lived in luxury but it was a gilded cage without freedom. Only a year ago she'd come to the conclusion that she should hand herself to God and work for Him. The nuns who'd tried so hard to educate her at the convent school lived a simple, peaceful life. She loved them all and still spent plenty of time with them. Her father would have been delighted to have a nun for a daughter. After all, Claudia was named after a vestal virgin. In the end, Imma had talked her out of it. She would be joining for the wrong reasons. Claudia loved

God but taking vows should be a vocation, not an escape. It would be wrong.

This marriage would be an escape too but her feelings for Ciro were so strong that it couldn't be wrong, could it?

Finally, she would have freedom from her father's all-seeing eyes. It was a shame that she'd spent little time with Ciro since his proposal but he'd been incredibly busy with his business, working hard to clear his diary for the wedding and their honeymoon.

Imma, keeping her hold on Claudia's hair steady, leaned forward to place a kiss on her cheek. 'I know you love him and I don't want to put doubts in your mind—I'm just being over-protective. I worry about you.'

'You always worry about me.'

'It's part of the job of being your big sister.'

Their eyes met again in the mirror and in that look Claudia knew they were both thinking of their mother. She'd died when Claudia was three. Imma, only eight years old herself at the time, had taken on the role of mother. It was Imma who had cuddled her when she cried, Imma who'd cleaned her childhood cuts and grazes and kissed them better, Imma who'd taught her the facts of life and prepared her for the physical changes adolescence would bring. There was no one in the world Claudia loved or trusted more than her sister.

Visibly shaking off the brief melancholy, Imma put the last pin in Claudia's hair. 'It's just as well you're sure about Ciro after all the money Papà's spent on the wedding.'

They both laughed. Their father's love of spending money was legendary but for Claudia's wedding he'd outdone himself. Insisting on footing the bill for it, in the space of five weeks he'd overseen what would undoubtedly go down as the Sicilian wedding of the century. Claudia had woken in her childhood bed that morning to the sound of a helicopter landing on her father's private helipad. She'd looked out of the window to see five Michelin-starred chefs hurrying behind the huge marquee in which the wedding celebrations would take place. Behind that marquee and out of her eyesight was another marquee that had been turned into a kitchen fit for an army of top chefs—another three helicopters dropped the rest of them off shortly after—to create the wedding banquet of which dreams were made and the evening buffet that would follow.

Claudia would have been content to have a simple wedding but had gone along with her father's plans to turn it into an extravaganza because it made him happy. Ciro hadn't minded either, content to go along with whatever she wanted, and so that had settled it.

As much as it made her all fluttery inside to know that for this one day she would be the princess her father had always proclaimed her to be, the greatest excitement came from knowing that in a few short hours she would be Ciro's wife.

She would be free…

Ciro walked through the villa's garden to the private chapel at the back with his brother.

'How much of his blood money has he spent on this?' Vicenzu muttered under his breath.

'Millions.'

They exchanged a secret smile.

Ciro still had trouble believing how easily his plan had knitted together. He'd assumed it would take months before he could propose with a good degree of certainty that Claudia would say yes but by the end of their first date she'd been like a puppy eating out of his hands. Cesare had been less than subtle about his wish for Ciro to marry her. He didn't know whether it had been father or daughter who'd been the keenest for them to marry. Cesare's insistence on paying for the entire thing had been too delicious for Ciro to put up more than a half-hearted effort to get him to change his mind.

Cesare's vast extravagance on this sham of

a wedding meant Ciro did not have to fake his smiles. Every step taken through the villa's transformed garden felt lighter than the last. Vengeance took many forms, some more palatable than others.

Another helicopter delivering another batch of guests flew overhead when they reached the chapel. The sound of rotors had been a background noise for the past hour.

The chapel too had been spruced up for the occasion. The white exterior had been freshly painted while inside the long wooden pews had been re-varnished, the stained-glass windows scrubbed and every religious artefact polished. When they entered it, the opera singer flown in from New Zealand to sing while Claudia walked up the aisle was performing vocal exercises accompanied by a world-famous pianist.

Before long, the chapel was filled with people there to witness the happy union between Ciro and Claudia. He cast his eyes around, satisfaction filling him. These people were the people Cesare held most dear, the people he loved to throw his weight around with and the people he wanted to impress. Once Vicenzu had fulfilled his part of their vengeance, all these people would know Cesare had thrown his money on a sham. And if there was a nagging sense of guilt lining Ciro's guts at his pretence, one look at his mother overrode it.

She sat in the front row next to his aunt. They'd flown in earlier that morning from Florence, their arrangements the only aspect of the day Ciro hadn't let Cesare control. Grief had marked her previously youthful, happy face with lines that would be permanently etched into her skin. She'd been surprised at his sudden intention to marry but too heartsick to ask any questions. Even if his intentions towards Claudia had been genuine, he doubted his mother would have had the emotional energy to invest in the ceremony as anything more than a spectator. There had been mild surprise that Ciro was marrying the daughter of her husband's childhood nemesis but other than that, nothing. Their father's lawyer had been correct—their father had kept the sabotage he'd received at the hands of Cesare's hired thugs to himself. His mother had been unaware of the immense pressure her husband had been put under. Ciro and Vicenzu were of the opinion to never tell her.

When this was done, once Claudia signed the family estate over to him as she'd promised— God, how easy was this? The suggestion had even come from her!—he might consider nominating himself for an acting award.

She'd kept up the naïve, unspoilt, wide-eyed

act beautifully too. No doubt she was waiting for his ring on her finger before showing her true nature. She'd been a little too thrilled at his marriage proposal, given after he'd asked her father's permission. Cesare had pretended to mull it over but Ciro had read the delighted dollar signs in his greedy little eyes. They had both agreed, at Ciro's suggestion, that a joint business venture should be put on the back burner until after the wedding.

It would be put on the back burner for ever. Only when Vicenzu got the business back for them too would their vengeance be complete. Only then would they confront Cesare and his daughters with the truth and watch the dawning realisation that they'd been played at their own game but that this time the Buscettas had lost.

A sudden buzz permeated the chapel's air. The bride had arrived.

Exactly on cue the double doors opened and the opera singer expelled the first note of her aria.

Such was his loathing towards Cesare that Ciro's attention was initially fixed on him, beaming like a fat peacock as he slowly walked his daughter down the aisle.

And then he looked at his bride.

Her face was veiled behind white Sicilian lace held in place by a diamond tiara. Her white dress was the dress of a princess, exactly as her father purported her to be. Heart shaped around the cleavage with small lace sleeves off the shoulder, it puffed out at the waist and formed a train held by her sister and five cute children he didn't recognise. Cesare had probably paid for them as he'd paid for everything else.

When Claudia reached him and Cesare melted away to take his seat, Ciro lifted the veil. What he found there…

In an instant his mouth ran dry. The pretty woman had transformed into a ravishingly beautiful princess. Truly, breathtakingly beautiful. Those big brown eyes… It was like peering into a vat of melted chocolate. He wanted to dive into it.

Maybe it was because he'd lowered his guard as the plot he'd woven came to fruition but for the first time since he'd met her, the shackles he'd placed on his attraction to her broke free. Desire snaked through his loins and thickened his blood. And all he could do was stare…

Only the non-subtle cough from the priest brought him back to the present.

Their wedding Mass began.

Ciro hardly heard a word of it. He was too busy trying to shake off the strange, unwelcome feelings rippling through him.

This marriage was a sham, he reminded himself. One day in the distant future, when his thirst to experience life and build an empire had been quenched, he would settle down and marry for real. His future wife would be someone trustworthy, a partner with whom he could raise a brood of babies and lavish the same love and security on that his parents had lavished on him. His future wife would be the antithesis of Claudia.

Claudia was the daughter of his enemy and an enemy of his in her own right. She'd been party to the dirty tricks that had caused his father's death. She was poison.

By the time they exchanged their vows, he'd got his body back under control and was able to look into the melted-chocolate eyes with only mild discomfort.

Superficial desire was the most he could allow himself. He needed his body to perform in consummating the marriage—he would not give Claudia any grounds to annul it—but genuine desire for a woman he despised? The thought was sickening.

The ceremony passed Claudia like the most wondrous dream. It *was* a dream. A dream come true. When they left the chapel to uproarious cheers, a pair of pure white love doves was released. Filled with happiness and wonder, she watched them fly away.

After the photos were done, the happy couple

and their one hundred guests made their way to the marquee for the seven-course wedding banquet. Another hundred guests would join them for the evening party.

The marquee's interior only enhanced her feeling of being in a dream. Luxury carpet covered the base while fairy lights crisscrossed the canvas roof, the entire marquee supported by Roman pillars wound with artful posies of roses. There had to be thousands of the beautiful blooms. And there had to be thousands of balloons too, of silver and gold, pastel shades of blue, pink and green, the colours blending together beautifully and combining with the roses to evoke an atmosphere of romance at its most opulent. The round tables were lavished with white tablecloths embroidered with gold leaf, gold cutlery and crystal glasses. Each guest was to sit on an elegant white chair…with the exception of the bride and groom. They were to sit on golden thrones.

Dazed, she accepted a glass of champagne from one of the army of silver-service waiting staff and, standing beside her handsome new husband, dazzling in a navy-blue wedding suit, greeted each guest in turn.

Unused to being in the spotlight, she left all the talking to Ciro. She hoped that in time some of his natural confidence would rub off on her.

Where did he get it from? Forming a multibillion-dollar business from scratch? Was it something that had grown over the years or something innate in him? Listening to him chat amiably to one of her father's business associates, she realised she knew very little about her new husband. Their dates had always been spent discussing the future. She'd avoided asking much about his past because she knew he still felt his father's recent death so keenly. Every time he was mentioned a shadow would form in Ciro's green eyes that never failed to make her heart ache.

A shiver laced her spine but she shook it off. This was her wedding day. She had the rest of her life to get to know her husband.

Ciro stood with his new wife and, hands clasped together, the flash of cameras showering them, they cut the exquisite wedding cake.

He'd enjoyed the day hugely and had played up his role of devoted groom. He'd made sure to cast long lingering stares at his new wife, to hold her hand at every available opportunity and even to spoon-feed her some of the berry *millefoglie* they'd been served for dessert. Pleasure had lit her eyes at this small intimacy, colour staining her cheeks when he'd followed it with a light kiss to her lips.

Ciro had decided it was better to keep his

hands to himself until they were married, in part to prove to Claudia—and her father—that his feelings for her were honourable and true, and in part to keep his focus where it needed to be. Claudia's easy acceptance of his work commitments had helped him keep the amount of time they spent together to a minimum. All they'd shared were a few chaste goodbye kisses, which had only added to his loathing of her. He despised how his senses reacted to the scent of her perfume. He despised that his lips found hers to be so soft and sweet. He despised how he could stare into her eyes and feel flickers of awareness deep in his loins.

And he despised how, as the day had gone on, the shock of desire he'd experienced in the chapel had snuck back on him and nothing he did could rid him of it.

The closer the time came to leave the celebrations, the closer the time came to consummate their marriage. The deeper the anticipation burned.

Claudia's ears rang with the applause and catcalls of their guests as Ciro's driver steered them out of her father's estate to the hotel where they were to spend their first night as newly-weds. Tomorrow evening they would fly on Ciro's jet to Antigua for their honeymoon. Her gorgeous new husband had made the honeymoon arrangements himself.

A warm hand closed over hers. 'Happy?' Ciro asked.

She met his eyes and smiled. 'I feel like I'm on top of the world.'

'It was a magical day.' Cheeks dimpling, he hooked an arm around her shoulders and pulled her to him. With her cheek resting against his chest, the strong thud of his heart beating against her skin, she inhaled his evocative woody scent then exhaled slowly.

Soon, very soon, there would be no clothes to act as barriers between their skin. It was a thought that had played in her mind constantly throughout the evening celebrations, unleashing butterflies in her stomach that had become more violent as the time for them to leave drew nearer. She didn't know if anticipation, excitement or fear had the greatest hold over her. Ciro knew she was a virgin. It hadn't been mentioned explicitly but then, it hadn't needed to be, no more than it had needed to be said that he'd had many lovers in his life. His experience meant he would know what he was doing and so making love should be as pain-free as it could be for her—at least, she hoped so—but his experience also meant her inexperience was likely to leave him disappointed. She wished she could have discussed it with Imma but, considering she was a virgin too, it would be akin to the blind leading the blind.

'Your father looked as if he enjoyed himself,' he said, cutting through her jittery thoughts.

She nodded into his chest and closed her eyes. Ciro's acceptance of her overprotective father was another of the many things she loved him for. She wasn't blind to her father's faults. He could be overpowering and intimidating but Ciro was comfortable enough in his own skin to let her father get his way without demeaning his own masculinity and Ciro had an easy charm that when he wanted things *his* way, he could put it across without it coming out as a challenge. She'd never imagined a man like Ciro existed.

She tilted her head and stretched her neck so she could plant a soft kiss on his lips. 'Today has been the best day of my life.'

He kissed her back. 'And mine.'

Soon they arrived at the clifftop hotel that would be their love-nest for the night. It was as opulent as everything else had been that day. Ciro tipped the porter who carried their overnight luggage up to the honeymoon suite, their other suitcases being held in the hotel's storage for their departure tomorrow evening and then, for the first time that day…for the first time ever…they were truly alone.

CHAPTER THREE

SHYNESS AND NERVES hit Claudia as starkly as the silence. 'This is nice,' she said, trying to inject brightness into her voice. Nice was definitely an understatement. Rose petals and tea lights in pretty glasses made a trail from the luxurious living area and through the opened double doors to the bedroom. There, an enormous four-poster bed draped with gold muslin curtains sat raised on a dais. More rose petals formed a giant love heart on the gold bedspread. On a glass coffee table by the sofas sat a bottle of champagne in a bucket of ice and two crystal flutes.

Ciro indicated the champagne. 'Shall we?'

'That would be nice.' She winced to hear herself use that insipid word again. Insipid—a word she'd learned only a month ago as part of her push to educate herself—was the opposite of how she felt inside. The butterflies in her belly now fluttered so hard they'd reached her throat and tied her tongue. Ciro popped the cork and poured them both a glass. When he passed Claudia's to her, some of the golden fluid sloshed over her shaking hand.

He raised his glass. 'To us.'

She chinked hers to it and spilled more over herself. 'To us.' Scared how croaky her voice sounded, she took too large a sip.

Green eyes held hers speculatively before he took the glass from her and placed it with his on the coffee table. 'You seem frightened.'

She swallowed and forced herself to hold his gaze. 'A little.'

A hand palmed her neck. 'You have nothing to be frightened of. We don't have to do anything you don't want or anything you don't feel ready for. If you want us to wait, then…'

'I don't want to wait.' She took a long breath. Waiting would only make things worse, give her mind even more time to play on her fears. And really, what did she have to be scared about? Ciro would make it special… Wouldn't he?

He gazed into her eyes a little longer before his dimples flashed. 'Let's take our champagne onto the balcony for a while. How does that sound?'

She managed to muster a smile through her tight cheeks. 'That sounds good.'

Fingers laced together, they carried their drinks through the bedroom and stepped through the French doors onto a large balcony that overlooked the Tyrrhenian Sea. A heart-shaped love-seat with big squishy heart-shaped cushions sat beneath an overhang covered in tiny romantic lights.

Ciro, having read the fear in Claudia's eyes when they'd been left alone in the suite, found himself dealing with a God-awful feeling of guilt. He thought back to his first time. There had been too much excitement for fear to get a look-in. But first-time sex was different for women and, as much as he despised her, he knew he had to be gentle. If he had to wait to consummate the marriage then so be it. Better to wait than scare her off sex for life. He wanted revenge but that didn't mean destroying her completely.

He held the train of her dress so she could sit comfortably, then sat beside her. Her rigid pose spoke volumes. For all that she said she didn't want to wait, she was clearly terrified.

He placed a finger on her neck. She stiffened further.

Hooking an arm around her waist, he moved her gently so her back rested against his chest. 'Listen to me,' he said. 'We will not do anything you don't want. We don't have to do anything at all. Any time you want to stop, you tell me and I will stop. Don't be afraid of hurting my feelings. Okay?'

She twisted to look at him and took a small

sip of her champagne. 'Okay.' Then she sighed and turned her face away to look back out at the spectacular view.

Draining his champagne, Ciro put his glass on the side table then carefully ran a finger over the plaits of her hair. Her wedding hairdo had held up beautifully throughout the day. He guessed having pins in it, however sparkling they were, must be uncomfortable. If he was to make this good for her—if they got that far, which right then he seriously doubted—he wanted her to feel as comfortable and relaxed as she could be.

He removed the top pin. It slid out more easily than he'd expected. One by one, he pulled them all free until the plaits fell like coils of silken rope down her neck. Satisfied all the accessories keeping her hair in place had been removed, he worked on undoing the plaits. The looser they became, the more the trapped scent of her shampoo was released. It was a soft, delicate fragrance that delighted his senses in much the same way her perfume did. When all her hair was loose, he gently ran his fingers through the thick mane that was as silken to his touch as to his eyes then kneaded his fingers over her skull. More of the delicate scents danced through his airwaves. Burying his face in the soft tresses, he filled his lungs completely. 'I love your hair,' he murmured.

Claudia, who'd found her fears slowly melting at his tender ministrations, twisted to look at him. His was a tone she'd never heard from him before, somehow more heartfelt than his declarations of love for her...

'I love *you*,' she whispered.

Green eyes held hers. The firm mouth flattened then loosened before he slid an arm around her waist to secure her against him and press his lips to hers. If he'd lunged at her with one of those hard, demanding kisses she'd seen in movies she likely would have recoiled in fright, but his kiss was gentle and caressing. When his tongue slid between her lips and found hers, her senses filled with a brand-new taste tinged with champagne that evoked thoughts of dark chocolate and danger. This was Ciro's taste, she thought in wonder; as intensely, headily masculine as the man himself.

Gradually, the kiss deepened. Tiny flutters of excitement awoke in her belly, muting the flutters of fear that had been there before. Secure against him, pressed into the crook of his arm, she placed a hand on his shoulder then tentatively wound it around his neck. His skin was warm beneath her fingers, the bristles on his nape like velvet.

When he broke the kiss, he rubbed his nose against hers. 'Don't move,' he murmured, rising to his feet. There was no time to question him for he hooked an arm around her waist and slid the other under the train of her dress. In one fluid motion, he lifted her into his arms, making her stomach plunge and then rise with the motion.

He stared into her eyes before giving a lop-sided smile that made her stomach swoon all over again. 'The groom is supposed to carry the bride over the threshold,' he said, then carried her effortlessly into the suite and sat her on the rose-petal-covered bed.

Her heart hammering so hard the echoes re-verberated in her ears, Claudia gazed at Ciro. This beautiful man was her husband. Her *husband*. It didn't feel real.

Palming her cheeks, he kissed her again. 'Remember,' he whispered, 'we don't have to do anything you don't want to do.'

Claudia wanted to thank him for his tender-ness and understanding but found her words stuck in her throat. Instead, she took a deep breath and pressed her lips to his.

'Give me a moment,' he said, stepping away to close the French doors, draw the heavy curtains and switch the main lights off. The flickers of candlelight illuminated the room in a soft glow that eased her fears some more. They softened Ciro's hard features, making him appear more human than god-like.

Standing only a foot before her, his eyes swirling with intensity, he removed his dinner jacket, tie and cufflinks and then, button by button, undid his shirt. He shrugged it off and let it fall by his feet.

Her mouth dry, Claudia stared at a body that rivalled any of the great Roman statues. Broad-shouldered and narrow-hipped, toned but not overly muscular, his golden skin was unblemished by anything other than fine dark hair around flat brownish-red nipples and lower down on his abdomen... A sudden burst of moisture quelled the dryness and she found herself sitting straighter, unable to wrench her eyes away, the flutters in her belly intensifying. And there was something else inside her too, a faint heat building low in her pelvis...

Ciro divested himself of the rest of his clothing bar his briefs. He'd sensed Claudia's fears slowly seeping away but when she'd caught sight of the outline of his erection, her eyes had widened.

Slowly. He must take this slowly. But, *damn*.

He knew his desire for Claudia was a little too deep for comfort but not for a moment had he thought he'd be here now experiencing a hunger he felt down to his marrow. Her kisses... As unpractised as they were, they *did* something to him.

He took her hands. Such pretty hands. The usually short nails had been extended by whatever women did to make their nails artificially long and painted a pale pink with tiny diamantes on the tips. A shudder ripped through him to imagine them scratching his back as he took her to the heights of pleasure.

Control it, he commanded himself. This, their first time together, was all for Claudia, not for him. Her pleasure was all he could allow himself to think about.

He tugged her to her feet and cupped her face to gaze into her beautiful large brown eyes. 'Are you ready for me to take your dress off? Or do you want me to stop?'

Her throat moved before a shy smile curved her pretty cheeks and she turned her back to him. Gathering her hair together, she piled it on top of her head and held it there.

Tiny clasps ran down the spine of the dress and it took him a few attempts to undo the first. The second came a little easier. By the fourth, he'd got the knack, but he took his time, pressing gentle kisses to the exposed flesh.

By the time he'd reached the clasps that ran over her bottom her breaths had become heavy and little trembles shook her slender frame. The dress now undone enough to remove, he pinched the sides of it and tugged it down to her feet. She stepped out of it and after a moment of stillness, turned around.

His heart caught in his throat. He closed his eyes, disconcerted at the strange feeling, but when he opened them and found Claudia's large beguiling eyes staring at him, the very foundations of his world seemed to shake.

Slender and softly curved, covered only in matching white lace underwear, she was ravishing.

He stroked her cheek. 'You take my breath away,' he whispered.

She swallowed and placed her fingertips to his chest.

His heart thudding so hard it felt as if it could thrash out of his ribcage, he gently laid her down and helped her wriggle over the rose petals until her head rested on a pillow. And then he kissed her. He kissed her mouth, rained kisses over her face and then slowly trailed his lips down her neck. The pulse at its base pounded hard.

Her skin was without doubt the softest and sweetest he had ever tasted with a scent that drove straight into his loins. In an effort to keep his ardour in check he tried to occupy his mind with things like financial reports, but the headiness of his responses to Claudia was too strong and all he could do was remind himself over and over to take his time and make this good for her.

When he reached her breasts she gave a sharp intake of breath and stiffened then almost immediately sighed and relaxed. Sliding a hand under her back, he found the clasp for the strapless bra and after a couple of fumbles undid it. Discarding it, he placed a kiss on one of the ripe nipples and heard her breath hitch and then a low, faint moan. Gently, gently, he kissed and caressed breasts that were much fuller than he'd expected and a hundred times softer.

The rest of her body was equally soft. Working languorously, he kissed, caressed and massaged her flat stomach, her gently rounded hips, discovered her inner thighs were a particularly sensitive zone for her, then moved all the way down to her feet. The only part of her body left unexplored was her most feminine part. She'd stiffened and automatically covered it with her hand when his mouth reached her abdomen and he'd known this would be a step too far for her. But he could smell her heat and it was as evocative and heady as everything else about her.

Claudia had had no idea pleasure could feel like this. Something deep inside her, something never before imagined or known, had come alive and it had spread into every part of her. Ciro's every touch heightened the sensations fizzing on and beneath her skin. There was a deep ache between her legs that burned and throbbed. For a moment she'd thought he was going to kiss her most private part and had had a brief flash of panic—surely people didn't do *that*?—but then he'd moved away and she relaxed into his tender attention and allowed herself to be enveloped by all the incredible feelings rushing and burning through her.

As his hands and mouth continued their assault of her senses, making their way back up her now boneless body, she hazily realised that her fear had disappeared. When his mouth found her breasts again, he trailed a hand gently over her pubis and touched a place that sent a bolt of sensation juddering through her, powerful enough to make her gasp and for her eyes to fly open.

What in goodness had caused *that*?

But then the wonderful weight of his body was on hers again and her mouth caught in a kiss filled with such hunger that all her thoughts became a cloud of Ciro. Something hard jutted against her inner thigh that made her insides clench then pulse even more strongly than before. She hadn't noticed him remove his final item of clothing…or hers. When he broke the kiss to stare deep into her eyes, she read the question in them. Her hand trembled as she palmed his cheek and lifted her head to kiss him.

His throat moved and he stroked her hair as he adjusted himself between her legs before sliding a hand under her bottom to raise it a little. The hardness that moments ago had pressed against her thigh was now right there…

With one hand holding hers protectively and their lips brushing together, he moved his buttocks. His hardness pushed inside her.

Claudia sucked in a breath and forgot to expel it.

He pushed a little further.

Dear *goodness*…

Her fingers reflexively tightened on his. She stared into his eyes. His jaw was clenched with concentration.

Bit by bit his thick hardness filled her. And, bit by bit, Claudia dissolved.

His gaze not leaving hers, he placed his elbows either side of her head and withdrew… only to slowly drive back in. And then he did it again. And again. And…

Dear goodness…this was incredible. Whatever had she been frightened of? This…this…

Sensations she'd never conceived of thrummed through her heightened nerve-endings, taking her higher and higher to a place she'd never known existed.

She melted into another of his kisses and wrapped her arms tightly around him. His chest brushed against her breasts as he continued to move inside her, a steady but increasing rhythm, every thrust taking her closer and closer to...

And then, just as she thought she'd found the pinnacle of pleasure, a flood of pulsations rippled through her, starting deep in her pelvis and spreading out through her veins; a riptide so intense that she found herself crying out Ciro's name and clinging to him, begging him not to stop, to never stop, never stop...

But even the most beautiful of experiences had to end and, just as she was floating back to earth, his thrusts became deeper, his groans longer and she realised he was about to reach his peak too. The moment that thought entered her dazed head, he gave an unintelligible shout and thrust into her one last beautiful time, holding onto his climax just as she had done, then, with a groan that sounded as if it ripped through his throat, collapsed on top of her.

For the longest time they lay there, his breath hot against her neck, her fingers stroking his hair, the only sound their ragged breaths and the beats of their hearts echoing together in her ear.

'I love you,' she whispered.

He lifted his head and stared at her. The expression in his eyes was unfathomable. But then he kissed her and rolled off, hooking his arms around her so she rolled with him and nestled into his chest.

Claudia drifted into sleep with more happiness in her heart than she had ever believed existed.

Ciro's eyes opened to darkness. Claudia lay beside him, an arm draped over his waist. Her deep, rhythmic breathing told him she was fast asleep.

He pinched the bridge of his nose and tried to get air into his tight lungs. He felt sick. He was especially sickened that he wanted nothing more than to roll her onto her back and make love to her again.

Damn it, it wasn't supposed to feel like this. He'd expected to feel like the king of the world. Not in his wildest dreams had he expected his plan to come together so quickly and so well.

Nor had he expected that making love to Claudia would leave him feeling as if something fundamental had shifted in him. He knew he'd made it good for her but all he felt was guilt. Her whispered words of love before they'd fallen asleep had contained such sincerity that he'd known he could never say them again to her because they weren't true.

He was going to break her heart.

Disgusted with himself, he carefully extracted himself from under her arm and climbed out of bed.

The champagne they'd shared still sat on the

coffee table, the bottle two-thirds full. He lifted it to his lips. It had gone flat, but he didn't care and drank deeply.

Not feeling in the slightest bit better, he padded quietly back to the bedroom, bottle in hand, and pulled his phone from his jacket pocket. Checking that Claudia was still asleep, he carefully drew back the heavy curtain enough to open the French door and step onto the balcony. He didn't notice he failed to close the door properly. It swung back open a couple of inches.

Resting an arm on the balustrade, he called his brother. It went to voicemail. Not unexpected considering it was the middle of the night.

'Vicenzu, it's me,' he said. 'Look… I can't do this for much longer. I've fulfilled my part. She's going to sign the house over to me today. You need to get your side done, and quickly. Whatever it takes to get the business back, do it, because I don't know how much longer I can keep the pretence up.'

Disconnecting the call, he swigged the last of the champagne.

It was the shift in the air that woke Claudia. She groped her hand over the mattress and found it empty. Scents she'd never known before filled her senses. Hazily, she realised it was the scent of their lovemaking.

About to call out to Ciro, she noticed the curtains had been drawn back a little, the French door ajar. She got out of bed, intending to join him, but as she reached the door his deep rich voice cut through the clear night air and seeped through the gap.

She heard every word.

CHAPTER FOUR

'ARE YOU SURE you're feeling okay?'

After a day spent being pampered in the hotel's spa, they'd returned to their suite. Claudia had immediately put the television on and curled up on the sofa.

She barely lifted her eyes to look at him and give the same answer she'd given every other time he'd asked. 'I'm a little tired.'

'Shall I order you a coffee?'

She glanced at her watch and shook her head.

Ciro had imagined waking on the morning after their wedding to find Claudia pressed against him, soft words of love ready to spill from her lips. The reality had been he'd woken alone and found her in the suite's living area, fully dressed, watching television and drinking coffee. 'Oh, good, you're up,' she'd said with a smile that wasn't quite as wide as normal. 'I'm *starving.*'

He'd offered to order room service, but she'd

been insistent that she wanted to eat breakfast in the hotel restaurant. When he'd leaned down to kiss her good morning her response had been a brief brush of her lips to his before she'd jumped to her feet with another smile and bounded to the bathroom. She'd locked the door behind her.

His imaginings that their day would be spent with Claudia holding onto his hand and planting kisses to his lips every other minute had been disabused too. She'd booked herself in for so many spa treatments that he'd seen hardly anything of her. To Ciro's disquiet, it had been *him* living in a near-constant state of arousal, him unable to tear his eyes away from her beautiful face in those times he actually saw her, him who ached to carry her back to their suite, lock the door and spend the hours before their flight making love. Claudia's body language told him clearly that she had no interest in doing that.

He kept telling himself that she was probably on a bit of a low after the high of the wedding and feeling overwhelmed by everything. She'd been a virgin. It could simply be that she was feeling a little sore.

He opened the minibar and found the bottle of bourbon he'd requested. 'Do you want one?'

She shook her head and pulled her knees up to rest under her chin.

'Claudia?'

'What?'

'There's something wrong. I know there is. Tell me.'

Dark brown eyes locked on his briefly before fixing back on the television. Was that *contempt* he'd seen flash at him? The disquiet that had been gnawing at him all day grew.

He downed a large measure of bourbon then crossed the room to kneel before her. Taking her hands in his, he stared at her, silently willing her to look at him.

'Talk to me,' he urged. 'Tell me what you're thinking. Did I hurt you last night? Are you worried about us not using contraception?' That had been a mistake he'd kicked himself for ever since. He'd been so concerned about making it good for her and so caught up in the moment that, for the first time in his adult life, contraception had been the last thing on his mind. He could only pray it wasn't a mistake that came back to haunt him. A child had no place in this sham of a marriage.

And yet, even though his marriage wasn't real, even though he despised her, he found her aloof, silent treatment unbearable.

When she continued to ignore him, he let go of her hands to grab the remote and turn the television off.

Her jaw clenched. She looked again at her

watch, looked up at him, looked back at her watch, lowered her knees to straighten herself then looked him straight in the eye. 'Yes, you hurt me and yes, I'm worried that we didn't use contraception. No child deserves to be born into a lie.'

Claudia felt no satisfaction to see Ciro recoil or the horror-struck comprehension rise on his face. She'd waited thirteen hours to confront the lying creep. All day she'd had to listen to him repeat 'are you okay?' and watch him giving her all those fake concerned looks, all the while resisting the urge to scream in his face and pound her fists against his chest.

All the tenderness he'd shown her, all the loving caresses, all the passionate kisses…

None of it had been real.

She'd stood by the French doors for an age, brain frozen, limbs immobile, the shock of what she'd heard and the implications too much to process. Then the paralysis had abated and, her heart hurting, she'd crept back into bed, trying desperately to think coherently. Ciro's words had played like a reel in her head. Her stomach had plummeted too, to remember the sparks that had flown between Imma and Vicenzu at the wedding. She needed to warn her sister. Get her advice. Try and make sense of what her heart so longed to deny but which the rational part of her head would not.

Ciro didn't love her.

When he'd eventually come back to bed, champagne fumes wafting from his pores, she'd feigned sleep and waited for him to fall into slumber before slipping out of bed and taking her phone to the bathroom. To play safe and drown out the murmur of her voice, she'd switched the fan on.

She didn't know how Vicenzu planned to take the business from Imma but, if his brother was anything to go by, he would have no scruples in getting what he wanted. From the shock in Imma's voice, Vicenzu's plan had already been set in motion. Claudia had promised to wait until four p.m. before confronting Ciro. This would give Imma time to come up with her own plan of attack before Ciro could warn his brother that they knew.

The thirteen hours she'd spent waiting to confront him had been the longest she'd endured. The hands of her watch had turned with the speed of a snail on sleeping pills. At least that was one thing she could read, she thought bitterly. She couldn't read words or men but she could read a watch.

But those thirteen hours had given her time to think and prepare. As humiliating as it was to admit, Claudia had been a doormat all her life. She'd been too frightened of the darkness in her father to speak out or stand up for herself, no matter how loudly she'd screamed inside.

She'd thought marriage to Ciro would free her from tyranny but all she'd done was exchange one hell for another.

The longer the day had gone on, the more the cold shock of Ciro's despicable betrayal had turned into hot fury. It needed an outlet. She'd thought of her favourite heroine, Elizabeth Bennet, and asked herself what she would do in this situation. Elizabeth would steel her spine and confront it head-on. And so must she.

A favourite line from Elizabeth rang in her head.

My courage always rises at every attempt to intimidate me.

It was a line Claudia always thought of with longing, wishing she had such courage. From now on it would be her mantra.

Ciro got to his feet and walked nonchalantly back to the bottle of bourbon. 'I'm sorry if I hurt you last night,' he said, his voice as steady as the hand that poured himself another measure. 'I tried to be gentle.'

'I'm not talking about sex.' She managed a

small laugh while inside her heart wept to remember how wonderful his lovemaking had been. What she'd thought of as the most beautiful experience of her life had been tainted for ever. 'Although remembering that hurts me too.' She swallowed. 'You should be ashamed of yourself.'

His throat moved before he downed the measure. 'I am ashamed. I should have remembered to use a—'

'Shut up.'

Ciro closed his eyes. Claudia hadn't raised her voice but those two words were delivered with a punch that landed right in his stomach. Every curse he knew flew through his head as the nagging worry that had played in his gut all day rose to the surface. She knew.

'I heard you. Last night. When you crept out on the balcony.'

'What do you think you heard?'

'Don't bother trying to gaslight me. I *know* what I heard.' Her eyes flashed as she casually mimicked, *"Vicenzu, it's me. I can't do this for much longer. I've fulfilled my part. She's going to sign the house over to me today. You need to get your side done, and quickly. Whatever it takes to get the business back, do it, because I don't know how much longer I can keep the pretence up."'*

His mouth dropped open. Ciro couldn't remember the exact words he'd said in the message he'd left for his brother but was pretty sure she'd just recited them verbatim.

She leaned forward and rested her elbows on her thighs. 'Why?'

He stared at her, head spinning, wrong-footed and taken completely off guard.

'Let's not waste time with more lies,' she said into the dumbstruck silence. 'I've spent the day hiding my feelings and I don't think I can bear to breathe the same air as, you a minute longer. You disgust me. But before I go, I want to know why you went to all this trouble. You married me to get your family home back, your brother is planning to get your family business back from my sister… Why? If you didn't want your father to sell them, why not buy them yourself? It's not as if you can't afford it.'

'Claudia…'

'Don't *Claudia* me.' Her voice was like ice. 'Either you tell me this minute why you've married me for a *house*, of all things, or I'm going to call my father and ask him.'

Ciro shook off the stupor that had caught him in its net and hardened himself. Claudia might have been a virgin in the bedroom but no child of Cesare Buscetta could be called an innocent. 'Cut the act, Princess, and stop pretending you don't know exactly what your father did.'

Her brow knotted.

'Let me refresh your memory.' He stepped casually towards her, his words slow and deliberate. 'Your father approached my father in January with an offer to buy the business and the family estate. Papà said no. He didn't want to sell. The business had been in the Trapani family for generations and he wanted it to stay that way, and he wanted to grow old with my *mamma* in the house where they'd raised their children. Your father wouldn't accept no for an answer and resorted to sabotage to get what he wanted.'

'Liar.' Her denial came out as a whisper.

He crouched down to look into the dark eyes ringing with an excellent attempt at confusion. 'Your father was the puppeteer in the background pulling the strings that entangled my father so tightly he couldn't escape. Papà was on the verge of losing everything, and then your father swooped back in like a black-hearted knight with his derisory, his *insulting*, new cash offer. It was barely enough for my father to pay off the debts your father's sabotage had heaped on him. Papà had no choice but to sell the business that had been in the family for generations and the home he'd spent his entire married life in just so you and your precious sister could have a property and a business that was legal.'

He laughed loudly, right in her face. 'Because, Princess, that's the kicker. The business and property sale were both legal. Your father made very sure not to get his hands dirty on this particular deal but only because he didn't want the stain to reach his precious princesses. He had no need to use guns or threats to get his way when good old-fashioned sabotage followed by a heroic rescue act worked so well. When I visited your father the day I met you, do you know what he said?' He moved his face close enough to see the flecks of gold in the darkness of her eyes. 'He said *nothing* about it. To him, it was insignificant. To your father it was just business. If ruining my parents' lives meant anything to him he would have refused me entry into his home and quadrupled the guards he posted on you and your sister. But it didn't mean anything to him. He wanted a nice clean home and a nice clean business for his precious princesses. He got what he wanted and moved on. But I can't move on.'

The colour on Claudia's golden skin had drained from her face. Her eyes were wide and dazed, her mouth opening and closing but no sound coming out.

Straightening, he cast her a look of pure disdain. 'Look at you, sitting there, pretending to be shocked at all this. *You* signed those deeds transferring the ownership of the house to you, *you* signed them, *you* saw the pathetically low sale figure that had been placed on it, *you* saw the state my father was in and still you signed it. A day later he was *dead*.'

He walked back to the bar but at the last moment resisted pouring himself another drink. He needed to keep his head clear while he considered the best way to handle this situation.

What the hell had he been thinking making that call to Vicenzu? All he'd had to do was keep up the happy and in-love act for a few more months at most. Idiot! Claudia hadn't signed the house over to him yet. His twilight call of guilt-laced desperation to his brother had ruined everything.

Leaning against the wall, he folded his arms across his chest as he faced her. He would not allow himself to soften at the shock that had seemingly enveloped her. He would not allow himself to feel guilt for the woman whose actions had contributed towards his father's death. 'Cat got your tongue, Princess? Must be hard for you, finding yourself on the receiving end of the fraudulent, immoral behaviour your family's so famous for.'

Long dark lashes shadowed her face as she blinked slowly. A solitary tear ran down her cheek but when she spoke, her voice was calm. 'I never met your father. I signed my part of the deeds with my father's lawyer. I knew nothing of…' She squeezed her eyes shut and inhaled deeply through her nose. 'What's the point? You won't believe me.' Her eyes snapped back open and fixed on him like lasers. 'Actually, I don't care if you believe me. What you have done to me is sick.'

She jumped to her feet and hurried to the bedroom where she grabbed her overnight case and threw it onto the bed.

'What are you doing?' If she thought she could leave and go running back to Daddy she had another think coming. Ciro had no idea how he could prevent it but he would try…

'You want the house so much, you can have it.' Her fingers struggled to co-operate but finally Claudia managed to unzip the case and remove the deeds that had been prepared for her by Ciro's lawyer.

The nausea crashing in her stomach was so strong she feared she might vomit right here and now.

Dear heaven, she believed him. All day her mind had whirled with questions. As Imma had pointed out, Ciro could have bought the house and the business with the daily interest he received. Why marry her for it? It had to be about more than bricks and mortar. In the back of her mind had been the terrible, disloyal thought that it was connected to her father.

He had no need to use guns or threats to get his way when good old-fashioned sabotage followed by a heroic rescue act worked so well...

Once, when Claudia had been very young, she'd run out of drawing paper. On a whim, she'd gone into her father's office looking for a fresh supply, a room she was expressly forbidden from entering. But her father had been away on business, the nanny busy doing something with Imma, the rest of the staff doing their chores, and Claudia had been too keen to get her little hands on more paper and draw more pretty pictures for a concept like consequences to deter her. She'd blithely rifled through the contents of his desk drawer but her short bout of rule-breaking had been brought to an abrupt halt when she'd touched something cold and metallic.

As young as Claudia had been, she knew a gun when she saw one. She remembered lifting it out of the drawer, remembered the heavy weight of it in her tiny hands and remembered the fear that had clutched her chest. The fear had been as cold and had tasted as metallic as the gun in her hand. She'd put it back where she'd found it and fled from the office, too frightened to tell anyone, even her sister, what she'd found. Did her father have a gun because he needed it for protection? If so, did that mean Claudia and Imma were in danger? Or did he have it because *he* was the bad guy? She didn't know and was too frightened to ask but the bubble she'd lived in up to that point had burst. She started paying attention. She listened. Hard. And she never disobeyed her father again.

Holding the envelope containing the deeds tightly to her chest, she stared at the hateful face of the man she'd stupidly believed herself in love with and plucked a figure from thin air. 'I want twenty thousand euros.'

'Claudia…'

'Twenty thousand euros and I'll sign the deeds.'

Disbelief shadowed his face. 'You're offering to give me the house? Still?'

She never wanted to set foot in it again. 'I want cash.'

'It's Sunday.'

'You think I'm so stupid I don't know what day it is?' she snarled. 'Get me the cash. You have half an hour.'

'Where are you going?'

She opened the door without looking back at him. 'To get the signing of the deeds witnessed. Half an hour, Ciro. Get me the cash.'

Fuelled by so much rage and humiliation that the pain in her heart was nothing but a numb throb, Claudia took the stairs all the way down to the lobby. After telling one of the receptionists what she wanted, the duty manager was summoned and agreed to be the witness. 'Where do you want me to sign?' he asked.

Thankfully, Ciro's lawyer had placed sticky fluorescent arrows on the pages that needed signing.

'You need to sign first,' the duty manager said, handing a pen to her.

There were two blank boxes with the arrows pointed at them. She peered at them cautiously, recognised her own name in the space next to the top one and placed the pen by it before hesitating. Embarrassment flushed over her face. 'Do I sign here?'

'Yes.'

She signed it carefully, using the same signature she'd used only months before when the same property had been transferred into her name. It sickened her to know she'd swallowed her father's lies so readily. Because they had been lies. She knew it in her heart.

But now was not the time to think too hard about it all. She needed to hold herself together a little bit longer and stay strong.

'Do you have my money?' she asked when she stepped back into the suite.

Ciro, who'd been sending messages by all different media to his brother to warn him that Claudia knew, working on the presumption that if Claudia hadn't told Immacolata yet then she would soon, shoved his phone into his back pocket. 'It'll be here any minute.'

'Good.' Walking purposefully to the bedroom, she zipped her case back together and carried it to the door, the deeds still tucked under her arm. Her eyes narrowed as she noticed him looking at it. 'You'll get this when I get my cash.'

He didn't like this hard side to her. It was the side he'd spent two months waiting to be revealed but now it was here in the open, all he could think was how little it suited her. 'What are you going to do?'

'You mean, am I going to tell my father.' Her face contorted. She opened her mouth to continue but a loud rap on the door cut her words off.

'That will be my man with the cash for you.'

She stepped aside to allow Ciro to open the door. He took the briefcase with a terse nod of thanks. Placing it on the table, he opened it, then stepped back so Claudia could look.

She stared at it for a long time. 'That looks like more than twenty thousand.'

'It's a hundred thousand.'

'Trying to buy my silence?' The look she cast him could have stripped paint. 'Count twenty thousand out for me. I don't want a cent more.'

'I'm not trying to buy your silence.'

'Just count the money.'

He complied, wrapping the crisp notes in a band. She snatched it from him and placed it in the handbag she had secured around her chest. When she next met his stare, the expression blazing at him could have dissolved the walls never mind stripped them. 'I have a cab waiting for me so I will make this quick,' she said. 'You are going to leave Sicily as we planned. Go to Antigua if you want, go to America, go to Mars, wherever you like, just keep away from Sicily. I don't want my father to know that you married me on a lie.'

'You want to protect *his* feelings?'

'No,' she spat. 'I'm not ready to face him yet with what he's done. I want to get away from all the lies and deceit because between the two of you, I don't know who I hate the most. If he knows I've left you, he'll want me to go back to him, so consider this a quid pro quo—you get the deeds...' she shoved them into his chest before sharply stepping back '...and I get the cash to disappear for a while. I will send him regular messages about how much I'm enjoying our honeymoon and the start of our married life so he doesn't worry that I've dropped off the face of the earth, so you need to keep your head down and keep away from Sicily. Got it?'

Ciro kneaded his temples. His head pounded. He was not a man used to being bested at anything but, in this, Claudia had turned the tables on him with meticulous precision. 'How can I trust you'll keep your word?'

Angry colour flared over her cheeks. 'How dare you? I'm the victim here. You told me you loved me, you married me, you made love to me and all along it was all a sick lie. If you'd told me from the start what my father had done, I would have signed the house straight back over to your mother.'

He gave a bitter laugh. 'You expect me to believe that, Princess?'

'Haven't I just signed it over to you? Look at the deeds—the house belongs to you now. Give it back to your *mamma*, do whatever the heck you want with it. I don't want it. It should never have been given to me in the first place.'

She picked up her travel case and opened the door. The speed with which she'd executed her plan was astounding. Ciro found himself in the rare position of being on the back foot of a game which he'd designed. 'Where are you going?'

'That's none of your business.' The door slammed shut behind her, only to fly back open again. 'If my father contacts you, you tell him we're delirious with happiness, got it? They're the kind of lies you're a pro at so I don't imagine it'll be a problem for you.'

'How long?'

'For as long as I decide necessary. I'll be in touch when I'm ready. Goodbye.'

CHAPTER FIVE

CIRO STOOD ON the balcony of his New York penthouse apartment and replied to his brother's vague message with an equally vague one of his own. The wind was picking up, bringing with it a chill. After the inhuman heatwave the city had lived through in recent weeks, the coming storm was a welcome respite. He doubted the storm in his stomach would receive any respite soon.

Five weeks ago, he'd been certain Claudia had told her sister about their plot but, with Vicenzu and Imma having since married too, he accepted he'd been wrong.

He'd relived their confrontation many times, remembering her facial expressions and body language, dissecting her words and actions. There was no getting around it: she'd been horrified to learn what her father had done to his. And she'd been horrified at what Ciro had done to her. The guilt he felt at this fought with the bitter knowledge that, innocent as she might have been of her father's evil games, she was still a Buscetta. She'd spent twenty-one years living with and learning from the monster. It would be impossible for his malevolence not to have seeped into her.

He'd had his lawyer check over the deeds. That had been no game or gimmick. She really had signed the house over to him. In theory, Ciro had achieved everything he'd set out to achieve. Vicenzu was also inching closer to getting the family business back—*why* hadn't Claudia told her sister? That was another thing he was no nearer to making sense of—but there was no satisfaction to be felt and no wish to celebrate. Not when Claudia had vanished off the face of the earth.

He couldn't stop thinking about her. Before their wedding his thoughts had been consumed with her father and his own planned vengeance. Now his thoughts were consumed only with her.

Where was she?

He felt as if he'd fallen into limbo, waiting for Claudia to surface so he could resume his life. He'd done as she'd ordered and kept his head down, quietly getting on with the running of his business. She'd stuck to her part too. If Cesare had any clue as to what had happened between them, Ciro would know about it. He would already have a bounty on his head.

He'd tried to call her but it hadn't connected. She'd blocked him.

After a fortnight the waiting had become intolerable and he'd set a crack team of private detectives onto finding her. They'd come up with precisely nothing. She could be anywhere.

Claudia sat in companionable silence with Sister Bernadette on the old stone bench. Around them, the nuns and volunteers who worked the convent gardens were picking fruit.

'I have to leave soon,' Claudia said. 'Tomorrow. I think.' As much as she would like to stay in this serene sanctuary, real life needed to be dealt with. Her time here, though, had not been wasted. She had learned much about herself and about her father. Questions she had never thought or dared ask before had been asked, and truthful answers given.

Those truths had broken her heart all over again.

Sister Bernadette gave a smile that perfectly conveyed her sympathy and understanding. 'We will miss you.'

'I will miss you too.' She covered the elderly nun's hand with her own. 'I cannot thank you enough for taking me in.'

'You are always welcome here, child.' Sister Bernadette gently squeezed Claudia's hand and got to her feet. 'I must prepare for vespers.'

Claudia watched her walk away feeling she could choke on the emotion filling her heart.

How she wished she could stay but it was impossible. Three weeks into her sanctuary she'd taken the test that had changed the course of her life.

She was pregnant.

Placing a hand on her still-flat belly, she closed her eyes and breathed in slowly. Now that the shock and pain of Ciro's betrayal had dimmed to a dull ache, her path was clear and real unfettered freedom beckoned.

After two weeks spent thinking and planning and channelling her literary heroines, she knew what she had to do.

She had to leave Sicily. Whatever happened, she would not raise her child here. Her father's reach was too great. She would be at his mercy—and so would her child.

She would never be at his mercy again.

And nor would she go running to Imma, not unless the worst came to the worst and it became absolutely necessary. She prayed for her child's sake that it didn't come to that. She prayed that she could build a cordiality with her enemy.

Claudia had thought a lot about her childhood

these last two weeks and how desperately she had longed for her *mamma*. She would never willingly put her child through that.

But from now on, she would be at the mercy of only her own decisions and choices. She would not be answerable to anyone. She would be like Elizabeth Bennet and take control of her own life.

As terrifying as it was, she had to go to New York and start a new life in the city her child's father called home. He had as great a responsibility to their child as she had and she would do her best to make sure he lived up to it.

Much as she wanted to take that freedom immediately, she knew she wasn't ready to live in a city as scary as New York on her own just yet.

Just reaching for her phone set her heart off at a canter. She spoke into it. 'Unblock Ciro.' Like magic, her phone unblocked him. She spoke into it again. 'Call Ciro.'

She only had to wait two rings before it was answered. 'Claudia?'

Her skin tingled and her throat closed to hear his rich voice. For a moment, she couldn't make herself speak.

'Claudia?' he repeated. 'Is that you? Are you okay?'

It was his fake concern that cleared her vocal cords. 'Hello, Ciro.' As she spoke his name, a fat bee landed on the lavender beside her bench. For some unfathomable reason, the sight of it made her smile. 'Are you in New York?'

'Yes. Where are you?'

'Sicily.'

'Really?'

'Yes. I want you to sort a flight to New York for me. We need to talk.'

'Has something happened?'

'You could say that.'

'I'll send my jet over.'

'A scheduled flight will be fine. I don't care where I sit.'

'I'll have you on the next flight out.'

'Make it for tomorrow. There's something I have to do first.' She disconnected the call before he could respond and breathed deeply to quell her racing heart.

Ciro paced the arrivals area of the airport surrounded by assorted people holding makeshift signs with random names. There was a family to the left of him, a father and two small children. From the excitement evident on the children's faces and their manic energy, they were waiting for their mother's arrival.

There was a manic energy in his veins too. It had been there since Claudia had broken her silence and called him.

As the wait lengthened—the storms currently hitting the east coast had turned flight schedules on their head—he found his attention lingering on that family. The life Ciro lived meant children were rarely on his radar. He'd always assumed he'd marry and have kids one day when he was ready to slow down, but that one day had always been far enough away for him not to bother thinking about. His gut told him he needed to start thinking about it right now.

If, as his gut was telling him, Claudia was pregnant, how could he reconcile being father to the grandchild of the man directly responsible for the death of his own father?

Agitated, he bought himself a coffee and had taken his first sip when a tranche of travellers emerged. Amid the crowd, dressed in slim-fitting jeans, a long blousy cream top and an artfully placed blue silk scarf, her long dark hair tied in a high ponytail, was Claudia.

Ciro's heart thudded against his ribs. His mouth ran dry.

Their eyes met.

Claudia ordered her suddenly jellified legs to keep going and tightened her hold on her overnight case and the strap of her handbag. It had never occurred to her that one look at Ciro would still have the power to make her heart flip over and her lungs shrink.

And then she was standing before him, gazing into the green eyes she'd once stared at wishing she could swim in them, wondering how it was possible she'd forgotten how deeply attractive she found him.

She hadn't forgotten. She'd buried it away, ashamed of an attraction that had been built on such heinous lies.

He gave a slow incline of his head then leaned down to pick up the case she didn't remember placing on the floor. The movement set off a waft of his woody cologne and for a moment the world spun as memories of their wedding night flooded her. They were memories she'd buried away along with her attraction for him.

'How was your flight?' he asked with overt politeness as they walked to the exit. 'Was there much turbulence?'

'Some. It could have been worse.' She'd been too busy worrying about seeing Ciro again to worry about the frequent bouts of turbulence they'd flown through.

'Have you got a coat? The weather's atrocious.'

She shook her head, not looking at him. She hadn't thought to check the weather conditions, had assumed New York would be basking in similar glorious heat to Sicily.

He put her case back on the floor and, keeping hold of his coffee cup, handed her the long black thing he'd been holding. 'Here. Wear this.'

It was a long waterproof overcoat. Everything in her recoiled at the thought of wearing something that belonged to him and she shook her head violently and thrust it back at him. 'No, thank you.'

His chiselled jaw clenched, the firm mouth forming a tight line. Then he picked her case back up and strolled out of the exit without waiting to see if she followed.

Hurrying after him, Claudia took one step outside and found herself instantly soaked by the deluge falling from the dark grey sky and almost knocked off her feet by an accompanying gust of wind. Only a strong arm wrapping around her waist kept her upright.

There was no recoiling this time, only a surge of warmth, which she had no time to analyse for Ciro had swept her forwards to a waiting oversized four-by-four, his huge frame shielding her against the worst of the elements. Moments later she'd been bundled into the massive vehicle. The door closed, muting the noise of the elements lashing down on them. Ciro, his dark hair flattened by the rain, his expensive suit drenched, tapped on the raised partition between them and the driver set off.

The car was warm and in no time at all the

chill from the downpour that had soaked her lifted.

'How long will it take to get to your apartment?' she asked, looking out of the window. Conditions were so bad she could see nothing but wet grey.

'With the weather and traffic as it is, hopefully no more than a couple of hours. I would have used the helicopter but in these conditions…?' His shoulders rose in a 'what can you do?' shrug.

A few, long minutes of excruciatingly uncomfortable silence followed until Ciro broke it. 'Where have you been?'

'In a convent.'

His burst of incredulous laughter sliced through her, laughter that stopped as quickly as it had begun. 'Seriously? You were hiding in a convent?'

'I needed a place where I could think and cleanse myself from your lies and my father's behaviour.' Twisting to look at him, she found her heart twisting too and exhaled slowly, placing her hand on her stomach, reminding herself of the need to remain strong and calm.

His breathing heavy, he took a while to respond. 'I apologise for what I did to you.'

'You mean marrying me on a lie?'

His head jerked a nod. 'I thought you were part of your father's plot against mine.'

She thought about that for a moment. 'We had an English nanny when we were growing up and she taught us that two wrongs don't ever make a right. Did no one teach you that?'

Ciro turned his head and found himself trapped in the dark depths of Claudia's stare. Every inhalation taken since getting into the car had found him breathing in her scent. It was the same perfume that had coated her skin on their wedding night and it coiled inside him, unleashing memories that had haunted his dreams ever since she'd gone into hiding.

He clenched his jaw and willed away the surging heat in his veins. 'What would you have done if our roles had been reversed? Wouldn't you want vengeance on the man responsible for the death of *your* father? Wouldn't you want to take back what had been stolen from you?'

Her chest rose, eyes narrowing slightly before she gave a slow shake of her head. 'I would never set out to humiliate or destroy anyone. I wouldn't involve anyone else. I could never live with myself if I hurt someone.'

'Then you're a better person than me, Princess. If someone hurts me or those I love, I strike back twice as hard. Steal from me and I will take it back with extras. Your father did both.'

'And how's your vengeance working out for

you? Do you feel better in yourself now you have your family home back?'

'I feel great.' To accentuate his point, he spread his arms out and hooked an ankle on his thigh.

The weight of her stare penetrated him for the longest time before a smile crept slowly over her face.

'Do you know, you are a terrible liar?' She actually laughed. '"*There are none so blind as those that will not see.*" I was so desperate to believe you loved me and so desperate for some real freedom from my father that I blinded myself. And deafened myself too.' Another short burst of laughter. 'If I had opened my eyes I would have seen the lies. If I had opened my ears I would have heard them. Your voice and body language tell the truth whatever comes out of your mouth.'

The proverb she'd quoted hit him. He'd been as guilty of it as she. The woman he'd believed to be stupid had, he realised, an insightfulness that saw right through him.

'What do you want to talk about?' he said roughly. 'We're not going anywhere so let's talk about it now.' The car hadn't travelled more than a mile since they'd left the airport. At the rate they were going they'd be lucky to make it to his apartment before nightfall.

'Haven't you guessed?'

His chest tightened into a ball. 'You're pregnant?'

She nodded. 'I took the test two weeks ago.'

'You've waited *two weeks* to tell me?'

'I needed time to think.'

'You should have told me immediately.'

She raised her shoulders and pulled a rueful smile. 'And you should have used contraception.'

He blew out a long puff of air and dragged his fingers through his hair. There was a painful roiling in his stomach similar to the feeling he'd had when he'd left his loving family in Sicily for a new life in America, but far stronger. There was no excitement amid the trepidation this time. Only dread.

He was going to be a father. He was going to be father to a child with Buscetta blood.

'You're okay with this?' He met her stare again. Claudia's calmness was as disconcerting as the news she really was carrying his child.

'That we're having a baby? Yes. I've always wanted to be a *mamma*.'

'You *wanted* this?'

Her face scrunched with thought. 'When our child was made I thought we loved each other so at that point, yes, I wanted a baby.'

'And now? After everything that's happened?'

'That doesn't change anything.'

'You still want it?'

'Of course. Don't you?'

He muttered a curse under his breath. 'How do I know what I want? You've had two weeks to think about this.'

'You've known since our wedding night we could have made a baby.'

'Having suspicions is very different from having facts.'

'Agreed. But you *have* thought about it.' She squeezed her eyes shut momentarily before fixing them back on him. 'I need to know if you can love a child that's the blood of your enemy.'

Her astuteness caught him off guard. Again.

'And please don't lie to me,' she added before he could formulate a response. 'Whatever happens in the future I will not accept anything less than complete honesty from you.' Her scrutinising eyes did not leave his face. If he was to lie, she would know…

'I don't know,' he finally answered. 'I never meant to bring a child into this.'

She pondered this for a few moments. 'Thank you for being honest.'

'How can you be so calm?' he asked, his incredulity finally reaching breaking point. 'I've lied to you, I've got you pregnant, I tell you that I don't know if I can love our child and you sit there as if we're discussing a new car.'

There was the faintest flicker in her eyes. 'Would you prefer me to rant and rage at you?'

'You're the one demanding honesty. That would be a more honest reaction than this serenity you're displaying.' Anger he could deal with. Anger meant he could shout back and displace some of the guilt that lay so heavily on his shoulders.

She pulled out the hairband holding her ponytail together. 'I've worked through my anger.' Her chestnut hair tumbled down. He remembered the scent of it. Remembered how it had driven deep into his bloodstream. 'You're the father of my child and I can't change that.' She massed the long, silken locks together and gathered them on her shoulder. Still staring at him, she continued, 'I can't undo the lies you told. I can't change *anything*. But I can influence the future and do my best to make sure our child has the best possible start in life that it can.'

His throat had caught. He had to cough to clear it. But, damn, she was plaiting her hair... and he was remembering all the heady feelings that had rushed through him when he'd unplaited it.

Damn it, he didn't want to remember. He wanted to agree a plan on how to proceed from this point, drop her off at his apartment then go out and get rip-roaring drunk. Alone.

'You're right,' he said, straightening. 'I *have* thought about what should happen if you're pregnant. As you're insisting on honesty, I tell you now that I don't want our child to be raised in Sicily with your father's influence.'

'I don't want that either.'

'You don't?' This from the daddy's girl who'd refused a date with him until she'd got her father's approval first.

He waited for her to elaborate but she continued plaiting her hair.

'I'll set you up in an apartment,' he said. 'If we live in the same city it will make it easier to—'

'For now, I will live with you.'

'What?'

She wound the band at the end of the long plait and jutted her chin. 'Only until the baby's born. I'll need support through the pregnancy and you're the only person I know here. I've never been to America before. I don't know the city. Living with you will give me time to adjust and it will give us the time we need to build some form of relationship that's not built on hatred. We don't know each other. All we know are the fronts we showed each other during our courtship—I'm willing to admit that I put on a front too.'

The air in the car seemed to have thinned.

'And how can you develop feelings for our

baby if you're not there to share the pregnancy?' she continued, clearly unloading all the thoughts she'd spent weeks developing while he was stuck playing catch-up. 'You're always travelling. If we lived apart I'd need to schedule time with you like we did before.'

'I don't want to live with you,' he said bluntly.

She didn't even flinch. 'I don't want to live with you either. Believe me, I feel nothing but contempt for you but my feelings don't count any more and neither do yours. I grew up without my mother and I've always felt there was a huge piece of my life missing. I don't want that for our child and I don't want it to be born with warring parents. You were prepared to live with me to get a house—are you seriously telling me you won't live with me for a short while for your child's sake?'

Ciro didn't answer. How could he live with this intoxicating woman even with an end date in sight? Every time he looked at her desire ripped through him but that desire was tinged with revulsion. He accepted that she'd been innocent of her father's criminally underhand activities but she was still Cesare Buscetta's daughter. How could he reconcile the two competing parts, the desire and the loathing, without losing his mind?

'I've spent two weeks thinking about this,' she said into the silence, 'and I think we both owe it to our child to try and find a way to get along in friendship rather than hatred. I don't expect it to be easy but let's give it until the baby's born.'

He breathed deeply. That was still, what, seven, eight months away? 'Live together until the baby's born?'

'Yes. We can look for an apartment for me and the baby in the new year and get it ready so I can move straight into it when the time's right, but for now we'll need to keep up a front that we're happily married. The last thing I want is for my father to think there's anything wrong with us until I'm ready to tell him. I've enough to deal with.' Her gaze penetrated him, burned him. 'But, Ciro...' She faltered before continuing. 'If at any time your heart tells you that you won't be able to love our baby, you must tell me. Our child is innocent of everything and I won't have it raised in hate. Better an absent father than a hateful one. If you tell me that I will leave and you will never have to see me or the baby again.'

CHAPTER SIX

THE RAIN STILL lashed Manhattan when the driver arrived at Ciro's apartment. Mercifully, a doorman with a giant umbrella appeared and held it over Claudia's head while she got out of the car. She could hardly see more than a foot in front of her but her other senses were working fine and when they hurried through the door she was ambushed by a really strong scent of perfume.

They strode through a small lobby to an elevator. Ciro placed his thumb on a wall scanner and the elevator doors opened. Not speaking or looking at each other, they stepped into it. Ciro pressed a button and they ascended, so smoothly Claudia hardly felt any motion. When it stopped and the doors slid open, she found herself stepping into another small lobby. Behind a horseshoe desk sat a wafer-thin middle-aged woman with a severe black bob and the most amazing, eccentric spectacles Claudia had ever seen, with rainbow stripes and small studded diamonds.

Ciro introduced them. 'Marcy, this is Claudia. Claudia, this is Marcy, my PA.' He made the introduction in English and then repeated it in Sicilian Italian.

He made his PA work in a lobby?

Marcy stood and shook Claudia's hand.

'I love your glasses,' Claudia blurted out in English.

Marcy beamed. 'So do I!'

Ciro put his thumb to another scanner beside a steel door then put his eye to a higher one. When both scans were complete, there was a noise like a puff and a green light appeared on the door itself. Ciro pushed the door open and held it so Claudia could enter.

It was like entering Wonderland.

'I didn't know you spoke English,' he said when the door closed behind them.

'Imma and I were raised by English nannies so we could be bilingual.' The foyer they stepped into had shiny black granite flooring, a Roman statue on a plinth, and stairs that wound upwards. 'You have two floors?'

'Three.'

'I thought apartments were one level?'

He grunted and led her through the open double doorway to the left that had the most magnificently decorated high plaster ceiling. 'Living room.' Back through the foyer and through the open door on the other side. 'Dining room.' He pointed to a door at the end. 'Pantry, kitchen and staff room.'

There was no time for Claudia to marvel at the grandeur of what she was being shown for Ciro had set off up the stairs laid with a beautiful hardwood that continued on through the long hallway. He opened various doors and barked out their usage. 'Gym. Library. Games room. Guest room. Your room.'

'My room?' She stepped into a beautifully appointed bedroom that was as high, bright and airy as the rest of the apartment. She'd expected Ciro's apartment to be dark and no-nonsense masculine but, while hardly feminine, it was tasteful and elegant, blending contemporary styles with Italian renaissance, not a single detail missed, right down to the hand-carved doors and the beautifully crafted window frames.

So this was how a billionaire lived, she thought in wonder. Claudia had grown up in a magnificent villa with extensive grounds but this was something else. Ciro's wealth made her father seem a pauper.

'The luggage you had couriered has been placed in the dressing room for you,' Ciro said. 'I didn't know what you wanted me to do with it. I'll get one of the staff to unpack for you when they come in the morning.'

She opened the door he'd indicated and saw her suitcases laid neatly on the floor. They must have been there since the wedding, shipped over in anticipation of her moving continents for the love of her life. Her heart clenched to remember the excitement that had filled her when she'd been packing for her new life…and then her heart stopped to see her wedding dress hanging on the open rail. She hadn't given the dress a second thought since leaving Sicily. Seeing it there, hidden away with the rest of her stuff, made her want to weep.

'Do your staff know we're married?' she asked quietly.

'I assume so. Enough pictures were leaked to the press of our wedding day.' Ciro looked out of the south-facing window at the bleak grey view. It matched his mood perfectly.

'Then we should share a bedroom.'

Every cell in his body stiffened.

She sighed. 'Ciro, like it or not, I am your wife. Married couples share a bed. What does it tell your staff if you put your new wife straight into a guest room?'

'Who cares what they think? They've all signed non-disclosure agreements.'

'*I* care.'

'We have enough issues without throwing sex into the mix.'

Her cheeks flared with colour but she held her ground. 'I never said anything about us…' she swallowed and managed to look both disgusted and dignified '…having sex. I don't want us to share a bed for *that*, not ever again, but we've been married for five weeks and not spent a night together since the wedding. For me to move in now and go straight into a guest room will look strange. I know pride is a sin but I can't help how I feel and I know that if I was to look your staff in the eye knowing that they know we're in separate rooms, I'd feel humiliated.'

A sharp ache pierced his chest at the confirmation he'd killed any feelings she'd had for him. He didn't *want* her to have feelings for him and wished he could kill the tumultuous emotions she evoked in him as easily.

'We don't have to share for long,' she added into the silence. 'A few weeks. Just for appearances' sake.'

'I didn't realise appearances meant that much to you,' he said stiffly, furious that she was neatly backing him into yet another corner.

'No one likes to be humiliated and I've been humiliated enough.' Her eyes narrowed. 'How were you going to play things if I hadn't overheard you? Where would I have slept? How would you have handled things?'

Knowing she would see straight through any

lie, he shrugged sardonically and plumped for honesty. 'I was going to install you in my bedroom then spend our marriage travelling without you until you gave me the house and Vicenzu got the business—'

'Install me?' she interrupted. 'What, like I was a bathtub or something? Isn't that the kind of thing that's usually installed?'

How could he answer that without sounding even more like a douchebag?

She folded her arms and pursed her lips. 'You don't even think of me as human, do you?'

'Of course I do,' he answered shortly. If he didn't have such a deeply human response to her they wouldn't be in this mess. If he didn't have such vivid memories of their one night of lovemaking he wouldn't be so reluctant to share a bed with her again, even if only for a few weeks. He was a man, not a machine, and Claudia was as hot a feminine temptation as he could bear.

Claudia stared out of the bedroom window, one of four in the master suite. The apartment's insulation and glazing were of such good quality she could hear nothing of the raging storm outside. With the dark night sky enveloping them, she could see hardly anything of it either.

Rubbing her arms for warmth against the sudden shiver that snaked through her, she drew the curtains. The silence was stark.

Ciro had gone out. Immediately after they'd shared a takeaway dinner he'd announced he had business to attend to.

Business at nine o'clock in the evening?

She hadn't bothered disputing this obvious lie. In truth, she was glad of some space away from him. She'd got her way about the sleeping arrangements. Ciro had carried her cases to the master suite himself. Her wedding dress remained in the guest room. She'd had a strong feeling he didn't want to touch it any more than she did.

His bedroom was surprisingly beautiful. The walls were painted a soft grey, the ceiling the same white decorative plaster as she'd seen in the living room, the curtains and thick carpet a soft shade of cream. The maroon duvet on the emperor-sized bed brought colour to the room, as did the tasteful colourful paintings of seminude women, which had not an ounce of sleaze in them. The overall feeling was one of peace. And she'd just bulldozed her way into Ciro's tranquillity.

Despite everything, she was proud of herself for holding her ground and not caving in.

The Claudia she'd been before the wedding would have rolled over and let him have his way.

Did he really think she wanted to be here? That she got any pleasure from forcing him to take her in? That she got pleasure from insisting they share a bed when the thought of sleeping beside him made her all twisted up inside?

She despised him for what he'd done to her but he was the father of her child. She could only pray that Ciro could bring himself to love it. She didn't expect him to forgive her father: forgiveness was something she was struggling to find herself. But she did expect him to forgive their innocent child for the accident of its birth. If he couldn't do that then he was not worth the effort of her trying and she'd leave without a second of remorse. If she could put aside her hurt and humiliation over what Ciro had done to her, then he could try too.

Too restless to sleep, she decided to explore the apartment properly. She remembered Ciro telling her during their courtship that he'd had his New York apartment remodelled a year ago to his specific tastes. What, she wondered, did his specific tastes say about him? She wasn't educated enough to say with any certainty but her exploration gave the impression of a man comfortable in his masculinity and his sexuality—there were lots of tasteful paintings and statues of nudes of both sexes—and a man who was tactile. All his furniture, hard and soft, had a touchable quality to it, materials chosen that were both aesthetically pleasing and pleasurable to the touch. It was an apartment that was a feast for the senses.

Back on the second floor and about to climb the stairs to the top, she felt drawn back to the library. Libraries were not Claudia's natural home and she tended to avoid them, but this one had the same feel to it as Ciro's bedroom. It surprised her that a man of Ciro's drive and restlessness had the patience to read.

She turned the soft lighting on and ran her fingers along the floor-to-ceiling bookshelves. Had Ciro read all these books? There must be thousands of them. She wondered if he had any Austen or Brontë on these shelves and figured it unlikely. She would give the clothes on her back to read their magical words with her own eyes rather than have to listen to them.

She pulled one of the books out and peered closely at the cover, trying hard to decipher its title. The effort made her brain hurt.

'That's a good book. You should read it.'

So shocked was she to hear Ciro's voice that the book slipped from her fingers. She hadn't heard him return.

Flustered, she quickly picked it up and slid it back where she'd got it from.

'Sorry,' she muttered, then felt her face flame

again when she looked at him. He was propped against the doorway. The sleeves of his shirt were rolled up, the top three buttons undone. The butterflies that had unleashed in her stomach on their wedding night awoke and Claudia became suddenly aware that she was dressed in her pyjamas. That they covered her from neck to foot didn't matter. Beneath them she was naked.

He stepped into the room. His thick dark hair was damp from the rain. 'Don't be. Books deserve to be read. I thought you'd be asleep by now.'

'Don't you mean you *hoped* I'd be asleep by now?'

She caught a faint glimpse of his dimples. 'That too.'

'Sorry to disappoint you.'

Being greeted by Claudia in a pair of silk pyjamas, her hair tied in two long plaits, could in no way be described as disappointing, Ciro thought.

Hoping to find some oblivion in the trusted method of alcohol, he'd met up with an old friend at a favourite bar two blocks away. He'd intended to get as rip-roaring drunk as he'd done in his university days and return home only when he was guaranteed to pass out. Four strong drinks in and the alcohol hadn't made a dent in his system. Six drinks in and he'd noticed a woman alone at the bar making eyes at him. She'd been extremely attractive with an abundance of cleavage on show. Three months ago he would have had no hesitation in introducing himself, buying her a drink and seeing where the evening led.

But that had been then. When he'd looked at the woman, all he could see was Claudia and suddenly it had hit him—in his desperation for oblivion and space from her, he'd left her alone in his apartment on her first night in Manhattan. Alone and newly pregnant.

Something sharp had speared his guts, bitterness had filled his taste buds and before he knew what he was doing he was throwing cash on the table for his share of the bill and bidding his friend goodnight.

What kind of a cold, selfish, heartless bastard was he turning into? That was the question he'd asked himself as he'd hurried through the storm back to his apartment. Part of him had hoped she'd be asleep, but as he'd climbed the stairs the sensation building in his loins and the fizzing in his veins told a different story. And that was the entire crux of his problem, he acknowledged grimly. His attraction for Claudia was at war with his loathing of who she was.

He shook his head. 'I'm the one who's sorry. I shouldn't have left you, not on your first night.'

'You probably did us both a favour,' she murmured. 'I think we both needed some space to breathe.'

He gazed at her, taking in afresh her slender beauty. Was he imagining that her breasts, jutting beneath the silken pyjama top, had grown since their night together? Did pregnancy work that fast?

Aware that his loins had tightened, he wrenched his gaze from her. 'How are you feeling in yourself? Healthwise?'

'I'm well. A little sleepier than normal.'

'Have you seen a doctor yet?'

'No.' She pulled a rueful face. 'My doctor back home is friends with my father. I didn't want to risk him telling Papà about the baby until I was ready.'

His stomach cramped at the mention of her father and it took all his effort to keep his voice even. 'When do you think that will be?'

'I told him this morning before I got my flight here.'

The cramping tightened. 'You told him before you told me?'

'I told Imma too, the day I took the test,' she said without an ounce of contrition. 'With my father... I needed to get it done.' Claudia squeezed her eyes shut. 'I didn't tell him I knew about the sabotage of your father's company or the other things I've learned about him since our wedding.

Not explicitly. Imma can deal with that when she's ready. But I needed to prove to myself that I could face him down.'

'What do you mean?'

Her throat moved before she answered. 'I knew that when I told Papà about the baby he would want me—you and me—to raise it in Sicily. I needed to look him in the eye and hold my ground and tell him our child would be raised in New York.'

'How did he take it?'

Her nose wrinkled. 'I don't know. I think I shocked him. I've never said no to him before. I laid it out to him then left before he could argue about it.'

About to delve into this further, it suddenly came to him what she'd said about her sister. 'What else have you told your sister? I was under the impression you hadn't discussed what you overheard me say to Vicenzu with anyone.'

Now something sparkled in her eyes and she covered her mouth briefly before saying, 'Ciro, I told Imma that morning after you'd crept back into our bed. I only waited all those hours to confront you so she had time to counteract whatever plot your brother had dreamed up.'

'But they're married now,' he pointed out. Immacolata was considered to be the clever Buscetta sister. If people underestimated Claudia's intelligence so greatly then how much were they underestimating Immacolata's? A woman like that wouldn't tie herself to a man she knew hated her.

'Their marriage…' She shook her head. 'All I will say is whatever you think about it is probably wrong.'

'Immacolata married him even though she knew the truth?'

'Yes.'

Ciro thought about all the vague messages exchanged between him and his brother since his wedding night. Ciro had deliberately kept his non-committal, his pride not wanting his brother to know that while he had succeeded in getting the family home back, on every other level he'd failed spectacularly. 'Does Vicenzu know that she knows?'

She sucked her cheeks in and covered her mouth again. Was she smothering a laugh…? 'You and your brother really need to start working on your communication skills.'

He couldn't argue with that.

Whatever she'd been smothering turned into a wide yawn. Her eyes widened. 'Excuse me.'

'Tired?'

She yawned again, even more widely.

'Not surprising.' He looked at his watch. 'It's

five in the morning in Sicily. You should get some sleep.'

She suddenly grabbed hold of the nearest bookcase and blinked a number of times. 'I was fine a minute ago.'

'You've probably been running on adrenaline.'

She nodded absently, still blinking, still holding on to the bookcase.

'Are you okay?'

She seemed to shrink. With a start, Ciro realised her legs were giving way beneath her. In three long strides he reached her and lifted her into his arms.

Her eyes widened, this time with shock. 'What are you doing?' Her voice had become a mumble.

'Carrying you to bed. Don't argue. You look like you're about to pass out.' As he spoke he carried her to the hallway then navigated the stairs.

Rather than argue, she rested a hand on his shoulder and pressed her cheek against his chest. Her hair tickled his throat, its sweet fragrance dancing into his senses. She fitted into his arms as if she'd been made especially for them…

She was asleep before he reached the bedroom.

Keeping a tight hold of her, he pulled the duvet back then carefully laid her down before covering her. She turned on her side and burrowed her head into the pillow, tucking her fingers beneath her chin.

Ciro couldn't tear his gaze from her. The longer he stared, the tighter his chest became and the more his fingers itched to touch her. His willpower broke before he even realised he was tracing a finger lightly over her cheekbone and then gently stroking the silk of her hair.

Then he closed his eyes and inhaled deeply before turning on his heel and leaving her to sleep. Alone.

CHAPTER SEVEN

CLAUDIA HAD NEVER been as disorientated as when she woke the first morning in Ciro's apartment. The room was dusky but light peered through the crack in the curtains…

She sat bolt upright, flames burning her veins as her last memory of the previous evening suddenly flashed through her. Exhaustion had swallowed her and Ciro had carried her to bed.

She noticed his side of the bed looked untouched. She clutched her flaming cheeks, bitterness filling her mouth as she realised he'd taken advantage of her exhaustion to sleep elsewhere. No chance of a comatose woman arguing with him about appearances.

Her mood lightened when she drew back the first set of curtains. The storm that had coloured her arrival in America a dismal grey had gone, in its place cloudless blue skies and dazzling sunshine. With wonder building inside her, she stepped out onto a terrace she hadn't noticed before. That wonder had nothing on the joy that lifted her at the view. Since when did New York have greenery? She'd thought it a sprawling concrete jungle but right in front of her lay a vast canopy of trees that must have stretched for miles... Was that a *lake* she saw in the midst of it? Yes, the greenery was edged by skyscrapers but to see nature blooming in the place she'd thought had eradicated everything that wasn't modern soothed her.

She walked the length of the terrace lined with brick flower beds filled with hardy manicured plants feeling that she was walking in a whole new world. It traversed most of the perimeter of the top floor and, even in the parts overlooked by other skyscrapers, remained entirely private. So taken was she with all the magnificence of everything that it took a beat for her to notice on her way back to the bedroom that Ciro had come out too.

Their eyes clashed. Her heart crashed. It took another beat before either of them spoke.

He looked up at the sky. The lines around his eyes crinkled. 'The weather more to your liking?'

'Very much. I'm sorry for oversleeping—I don't think I've ever stayed in bed so late.'

She caught a faint glimpse of his dimples. 'You needed it. Ready for something to eat?'

'Have I missed breakfast?'

'If you want breakfast, have breakfast.'

'Lunch will be fine. Is it okay for me to have a shower first?'

His brow furrowed, his eyes speculative. 'You're an adult, Princess. You don't have to ask.'

'I know...' She shrugged sheepishly. 'It's going to take a while for me to stop feeling like a guest here.'

'Sure.'

He didn't say anything about her *not* being a guest, she noted. 'Can you do me a favour?'

'That depends what it is.'

'Can you stop calling me Princess? It sounds like you're mocking me.'

He bowed his head. 'Sure. Take a shower and then we'll get some lunch.'

He didn't deny that it sounded like a mockery, she noted, glaring at his retreating back.

She followed him back into the bedroom. It didn't surprise her that he'd made himself scarce from it.

Ciro was on a call to his Madrid store manager when Claudia entered the living room.

Gone was the vulnerable waif dressed in pyjamas he'd had a short conversation with on his terrace. In her place stood a woman dressed in a loose cream V-necked top that skimmed her cleavage, smart figure-hugging trousers that rested above her ankles and a bold blue slim-fitting jacket with oversized sleeves. Her dark chestnut hair hung loose and gleamed in the natural light that poured in from the windows. Large hooped gold earrings hung from her pretty ears. Around her shoulders she carried an over-size handbag. She looked dazzling.

He sucked in a breath and immediately found his lungs assailed by her perfume and his loins tightening.

Damn but his attraction to her was acceler-ating.

He'd slept on the sofa in his library, thinking it a good compromise to sharing his bed. There would be no disarranged guest bed for his staff to notice and he could sleep without being dis-turbed too. It hadn't worked. His head had been too full of Claudia, imagining her asleep in his bed, remembering the softness of her skin, the swell of her breasts, the firmness of her thighs, all the things he should have banished from his mind, for sleep to come. It had been bad enough during those five weeks she'd dropped off the map but now she was here in the flesh, disturb-ing him on more levels than he could count. She hadn't been in his home for a day yet and already everything felt different.

Was it the allure of forbidden fruit causing it, his vow never to touch her again perversely making his desire grow? He'd assumed that making love to her once would be enough to sate that desire but the opposite had happened. The way he felt, he didn't dare even touch her.

'Ready to go?' he asked.

She nodded. 'Where are we eating?'

'I thought we could go to my restaurant for lunch.'

'You have a restaurant?'

'In the store.'

He led the way to the elevator, passing Marcy, who was on a call and lifted a hand to acknowledge them.

The elevator stopped two floors down and the doors opened. Ciro stepped out and waited for Claudia to follow.

She didn't move. Her eyes were wide as she took in the vast expanse before her. If he hadn't stuck his foot in, the doors would have closed with her still in it.

'*This* is your department store?' she asked, finally leaving the elevator.

'This is my flagship store,' he confirmed. 'The biggest of the Trapani department stores and the hub of my business.'

'It's *huge*.' Claudia had never been in a place like it. They didn't make department stores like this in Sicily. It wasn't just the size that stole her breath but the richness of the décor…the *beauty* of it all. 'That explains the perfume.'

'What perfume?'

'When we entered the building yesterday I smelt perfume. I wondered where it came from.' They were on what was obviously the homeware floor but the scent of perfume was still strong. 'I didn't know you lived above one of your stores.'

'I have apartments above all of them. It makes life easier for me.'

She remembered him saying he owned twenty-one department stores across Europe, North America and the Middle East and that he planned to open many more. 'But this is your main home, isn't it?'

He nodded.

They walked through the finely dressed shoppers bustling around them. Claudia's eye caught a display of quirky and beautiful vases. She leaned closer to look at a jade-green one shaped like a swan and concentrated on its price tag. The numbers were a blur so she counted them… Five figures before the decimal point! She stepped back sharply before she could accidentally knock it over.

Her eye was next caught by a display of top-of-the-range electronic food mixers with more attachments than she'd known existed.

'I thought you were hungry,' Ciro said, his voice bemused.

'I am but these are amazing. Look at this—it chops, whisks, blends, kneads and…' Her voice tailed off as embarrassment at getting as excited over a food mixer as a child got over a bag of sweets suddenly curdled in her.

'Tell me the colour you want and I'll have one sent up to the apartment for you.'

She shook her head and started walking again, following her sense of smell in the direction of warm food now wafting in the air around them. 'You don't have to humour me.'

'I'm not humouring you.'

'I can't afford it.' Her heart wrenched to remember all the baking equipment she'd left behind in Sicily, left when she'd thought she would return to them and use them every summer as a cherished wife.

A warm hand caught hold of her wrist and stopped her walking.

She twisted round and almost slammed into him.

Shocked at the blast of heat his proximity sent through her, she stepped back, only to barge into a passing shopper. Embarrassed anew, she apologised profusely. When she turned back to Ciro, she caught him wiping the hand he'd caught hold of her with on his trousers and her embarrassment tripled.

'I'm not humouring you,' he repeated, acting as if there were nothing wrong with erasing the feel of her from his skin. 'You can have whatever you like from the store. It all belongs to me. Take whatever you like from any floor whenever you like. I'll let the staff know.'

Further embarrassed to be made to feel like a charity case from an unwilling benefactor, she nodded, knowing she would never take anything from these shelves. She would let Ciro feed her and give her a roof to live under, but she would never take anything else from him, not when the mere touch of her skin repelled him.

She kept pace with him as they walked past a queue of beautifully dressed people snaking out of the restaurant door and into a room so plush and elegant that she gasped. The store's restaurant had to be a destination in itself.

They were led to a window table by a fawning waiter. Leather-bound menus were placed in front of them.

'Shall we eat off the lunch menu or do you want something more substantial?' Ciro asked.

'The lunch menu's fine.' When she looked up, he'd opened his menu and was peering through it. She pretended to study hers too.

'What do you fancy?'

'I don't know.' How could she tell him she couldn't read their own language, never mind a foreign one? He thought her stupid enough as it was without her confirming it for him. She'd been lucky with the few restaurants he'd taken her to during their courtship as the waiting staff had always recited the specials of the day and she'd always pounced on one of them as her choice. 'What do you recommend?'

He raised a shoulder but didn't look at her. 'It's all good.'

She closed her menu and pushed it to one side. 'Why don't you order for me?'

He lifted his head, a furrow in his brow. 'Has the fact it's the twenty-first century passed you by? Or are you too used to doing Daddy's bidding to think for yourself?'

Angry, humiliated heat seared her skin. 'That's offensive.'

He didn't look in the slightest bit chastened. 'You admitted last night that you've never said no to your father before. That implies you always do his bidding. You ask permission to have a shower and now you're asking me to choose the food you eat? That's the behaviour of a child. You're an adult. It's time you started acting like one.'

'I'd say putting our baby above my own feelings and being here with you means I'm already doing that,' she snapped back, 'So keep your character assassination to yourself.'

If she'd had any thought of confessing her inability to read or write, he'd just killed it. To tell him the truth would be tantamount to giving him a loaded gun to use against her.

Luckily, the waiter returned to their table to take their order. Ciro indicated for her to order first.

Managing a small smile for the waiter, she said, 'I'm in the mood for something light but filling. What do you recommend?'

Ciro smothered his annoyance. Claudia, he was learning, had a strong-headed stubborn streak in her, traits she must have inherited from her father, and as he thought this his mood soured further.

He kept telling himself that she'd had nothing to do with her father's plot against his, but while that was true she should have opened her eyes. Wilful ignorance was no excuse.

He drank some lemon-infused water and looked at her. She was staring out of the window, ignoring him.

A change of subject was needed. 'What do you intend to do to occupy your time before the baby's born?'

She turned her head slowly to face him. Long,

dark lashes swept downwards before she answered. 'I have no idea.'

'Are there things you've always wanted to try or do but have never been able to before?'

'Not anything in particular.'

'New York is a big, diverse city. I doubt there is anything you can dream of doing that you can't do here. You can finish your education. Take classes. Learn new skills. Anything you want.'

'I don't drive. Getting around will be hard for me.'

'There you go—you can have driving lessons.'

Her fingers tightened around her glass. 'I've had lessons. Driving is not for me.'

Ciro found his own fingers tightening too. For all her stubbornness, Claudia was a sheep. A follower. Someone who hung back, having no dreams, no plans or hopes for the future. He didn't understand how anyone could be that way. As his mother had said many times, Ciro had been born with fire in his belly. He'd been restless to leave Sicily and get out into the big wide world. He'd wanted to experience everything the world had to offer and make a name for himself. He'd succeeded beyond his wildest dreams. Claudia's apathy was alien to him.

'Most New Yorkers use public transport,' he informed her.

Her eyes widened. He detected alarm. He supposed public transport was beneath this pampered princess. 'Don't worry, I wouldn't expect you to mix with the general public. I'll have a driver put on standby for you.'

If he hadn't been watching so closely he'd have missed the almost imperceptible shudder she gave at the suggestion.

His irritation grew. 'Happy to spend the next seven, eight months just hanging around the apartment, are you?'

A flash of anger reflected back at him from the doe-like eyes. 'I've only just got here and already you're looking at ways of getting me out from under your feet?'

'It's not my feet you'll be under, Princess. I don't spend much time in the apartment—I've taken today off to help you settle in but tomorrow I'm off to Los Angeles for a couple of days.'

'I've asked you not to call me that. And do I assume that your trip means you're intending to deal with me the way you'd intended to before? Install me in your apartment and then run away so you don't have to deal with me to my face?'

'I'll be back by the weekend. We can spend all the time together you want then.'

'If you're just going to keep picking on me and criticising me then I'd rather not bother.'

'I'm not picking on you.'

'Aren't you? It seems that you're determined to find fault with me. You assumed I wouldn't want to use public transport because I have a dislike of the general public. How dare you assume that? I don't think I'm better than anyone else—I *know* I'm not.'

'I didn't mean it like that.'

'I've asked you not to lie to me. That's exactly what you meant. How can you get to know the real me if you keep making assumptions to suit your own prejudices? Do you have any idea how sheltered my upbringing was? I've never used public transport in my life! The thought of using it here in a city as dangerous as this—the thought of going *anywhere* in this city alone—is terrifying for me.' She looked back out of the window. Her jaw was tight, her throat moved, and she was blinking a lot…

With a muttered curse, Ciro realised she was on the verge of tears. Before he could even think of addressing it, the waiter brought their lunch to their table.

When they were alone again, she picked up her fork and stabbed a chunk of avocado.

Thankful she'd held the tears at bay—he was *useless* at dealing with crying women, even if their tears were of the crocodile variety—he attempted to moderate his tone. 'Where did you get the impression New York's such a dangerous place?'

She didn't look at him. 'From my father.'

'He told you that?'

A short nod and then the avocado disappeared into her mouth.

'I don't know where he got that impression from but it isn't true. It hasn't been true in decades. Sure, there are areas it's best to avoid but all cities have those areas.'

'He told me about it when I left school. I wanted to visit America and see all the landmarks from the movies I loved but he explained how dangerous America and the rest of the world really is.'

Blood pulsed in his temples to imagine her as a child watching the same movies as he'd watched and formulating similar dreams. The difference was Claudia had been all too easily dissuaded from following hers. Nothing on earth could have dissuaded Ciro from following his dreams.

'And you believed him?' he asked.

'Why wouldn't I?'

'You didn't think to do your own research?'

She gave a sharp shake of her head. Her face, he noted, had turned the same colour as the cherry tomato she'd just popped into her mouth.

'Do you just take whatever anyone tells you

as gospel?' he pushed, his disdain towards her growing. 'Five minutes researching crime statistics would have given you the truth.'

After a long beat she put her fork on her plate, her elbow on the table and rested her forehead in her hand. 'Ciro... Please, stop this.' After another long beat she raised her eyes to meet his. Sadness and defeat shone at him. 'I couldn't do my own research because I can't read.'

Ciro stared at her, wondering what on earth she was talking about. 'Can't read what? Off an electronic screen?'

'Letters. Words. I can't read anything.'

'What the...?' He cut himself off. He shook his head. He blinked. He shook his head again. 'What kind of joke is that? Of course you can read. I've seen you.'

'No, you haven't.'

'I have. In my library last night.'

'I was holding the book, not reading it. I would give *anything* to be able to read it.'

'But I've seen you read through menus...' And then his skin chilled as he thought back thirty minutes to when she'd asked him to order for her and then stubbornly got the waiter to recommend a dish when he'd refused.

And then he remembered how during their months of courting she'd always chosen from the specials board after it had been recited by whoever was serving them.

He shook his head again to clear the white noise filling it. 'But you're obviously well read. You can tell by the language people use. And you've mentioned books you've read.'

'Books I've *enjoyed*,' she contradicted softly. 'Imma introduced me to audio books when I was fourteen. I love listening to them.'

'But…' He swallowed. He'd known Claudia for over three months now. He'd married her. She carried his child. How could he not know something so fundamental about her? 'How the hell can anyone reach the age of twenty-one without learning to read?'

'I've recently discovered that I'm dyslexic. Severely dyslexic.' She bit into her bottom lip. 'I never knew it. I thought the same as everyone else that I'm just stupid.'

'You're not stupid.' That was one thing he could say with certainty.

She smiled wanly then picked her fork up and stabbed a prawn. 'I don't see letters as other people do. To me they're just squiggles. The written word means absolutely nothing to my brain. It never has.'

His appetite gone, Ciro pushed his plate to one side. 'Why didn't you tell me this before?'

She inhaled through her nose and stared back

out of the window. She spoke so softly he had to strain to hear the words. 'I was ashamed.'

'Of what?'

And then she turned her face back to him. Her eyes glistened. 'Of being illiterate. Men like you…'

'Men like me?'

'You could have married anyone you wanted. You were my only choice and I was desperate to marry you.' Her voice barely rose above a whisper. 'I had all these crazy feelings for you and I wanted the freedom you represented so badly. I was terrified that if you knew the truth you'd have second thoughts and call the wedding off.'

Ciro expelled a long breath slowly. 'What made you think that?'

'Because you're so successful and have such *confidence*. You're not scared of anything and anything you set your mind to do, you do it. Look at all this…' There was a spark of animation in her eyes as she made a circular motion with her hand. 'I can't begin to imagine how hard you've worked and the drive you needed to create it all. I'm only telling you about my dyslexia now because it's *horrible* knowing you think of me as pampered and lazy for not being career-minded. It's not because I don't want to be but because I *can't*, just as I couldn't dispute what my father told me about the world—I had no way to check even if I'd wanted to. Imma was at university so she wasn't part of the conversation and none of Papà's staff were going to contradict him. Technology has made my life easier recently and I have a voice-activated phone that can read messages and the pages of websites aloud to me but back then, I had *nothing*. I believed Papà because I had no reason to think he'd lie to me.'

Ciro's head spun, thought upon thought running through his head, guilt roiling his stomach. How had he not picked up on this before? Now that she'd told him, he could see all the signs he'd missed. Normally, he didn't miss anything but with Claudia...

With Claudia he'd ignored the signs because, as she'd rightly pointed out, he'd had preconceived prejudices against her and had used them to suit his preconceived assumptions.

'I'm hopeful that now I know the cause of my illiteracy I might be able to get some help for it,' she said after a long period of silence passed between them while Ciro tried to put some order to his thoughts. 'But please, let me adjust to my new life here first. This is all very overwhelming for me.'

He rubbed his temples and blew out more air. 'You should have told me before. You're the one who keeps going on about honesty.'

'I know,' she whispered. 'I was scared. I'm sorry.'

Something squeezed around his heart to see the despondency in her eyes and he found himself saying, 'I'll be in LA until Friday. How about we spend the weekend exploring the city and our neighbourhood together? It'll do you good to become familiar with everything and then you'll be able to judge for yourself if New York's as scary as you think it is.'

She considered this for a moment before nodding. 'That would be nice.'

'It's settled, then. And, Claudia… I'm sorry if I upset you. That was never my intention.'

Her eyes held his before she gave a sad smile. 'Wasn't it?'

CHAPTER EIGHT

CLAUDIA LAY ON the library's reading sofa listening to her favourite book being narrated through her headphones. Outside the closed door she heard distant voices and movement but as Ciro's apartment was currently filled with his cleaning staff, she didn't think much of it. In the four days she'd been here, she'd become as accustomed to their presence as she'd been when living at home. The one good thing was that Ciro's staff didn't live in. They came in daily to clean and sort the laundry and then left.

She'd spent the two evenings Ciro had been in LA alone. The first night had been strange and a little frightening. She'd never been alone before. Even the three months in the farmhouse had been spent with her father's security detail on hand if she needed them, her privacy an illusion she'd gone along with because it had been more privacy than she'd ever enjoyed in her life. She'd still been at the mercy of her father's bidding.

Being alone here felt very different. Ciro had left her the number of his concierge, who provided her with anything she required, but there was no feeling of being spied on, no one reporting on her movements…yes, it felt very different. But good.

The only downside had been her stupid mind's refusal to stop thinking about Ciro. After she'd told him about her dyslexia, nothing more had been said about it but she'd sensed a change of mood in him. Whether he thought less of her for it—if it was even possible for him to think less of her than he already did—only time would tell.

She hadn't told him for sympathy but because she'd realised that, without the truth, he'd continue seeing her as spoilt and lazy. It had been the hardest thing she'd ever had to say but she'd rather him think her stupid than think that.

Pushing thoughts of Ciro away for the fiftieth time since she'd laid down, she squeezed her eyes even tighter and tried to concentrate on Elizabeth's verbal sparring with Mr Darcy.

It took a beat for her brain to register the library door open then a further beat for her senses to register the woody cologne diving into her airstream.

Yanking the headphones off, she sat up straight and swung her legs around. 'You're back,' she said, then winced at the stupidity of her observation. Of course he was back. He was standing right in front of her, all tall, dark, brooding machismo.

The butterflies in her stomach awoke with as great a start as she'd done and set about on a violent rampage that in turn set her heart off on a canter.

How was it that every time they parted she forgot how devastating he was? And how was it that every time she saw him after a period apart the intensity of her reaction to him increased?

Aiming for nonchalance, she added, 'Sorry, I didn't think you were due back for a few more hours.'

Her heart jolted from its canter to see his dimples flash then accelerated at a frightening rate.

'I finished sooner than I thought.'

'Did you have a good trip?' She had no idea how she managed to ask that with the eruption taking place inside her.

Ciro shrugged. LA was his least favourite city and not a place he ever felt enthused about going to. Unless you were a social butterfly, there was nothing to do there. When he travelled for business he always liked to do something new outside business hours, something invigorating. 'It was productive. How have you been?'

He'd been disconcerted to find he'd been the one to call and check that everything was okay.

Only the one call, after yesterday's final meeting when he'd been unable to take the silence any more. After the tension during their lunch together and Claudia's shocking dyslexia admission, they'd spent the rest of the day in different parts of the apartment. He'd spent another night in the library. The tension had still been tangible between them when he'd said goodbye the next morning.

She nodded, perhaps a little too vigorously. 'I've been fine, thank you.'

'Good. I need to take a shower—I thought we could go out to eat. Have a think about what you fancy and… What's wrong?' Her eyes had swept away from him to stare at the floor.

Her shoulders rose. 'I thought you'd be tired after all the travelling and meetings so I made Chicken Cacciatore.' Then, more brightly, she continued, 'It doesn't matter, it'll freeze. I'll have it next time you're away.'

He could hardly believe she'd thought to cook for him, especially after the way things had been between them. And now he was thinking about it, he remembered catching the scent of cooking when he'd first walked into the apartment but the kitchen was far enough away from the foyer and the aroma of furniture polish had been strong so it hadn't really registered with him.

'When will it be ready?' he asked.

'It's ready now—it's keeping warm in the oven. I just need to cook the pasta I've made to go with it.'

'Great. I'll have a shower and then we'll eat together.' It took a lot of effort to keep the stiffness from his voice. From the moment he'd stepped into the library everything inside him had tightened, his body automatically waging war on itself. 'I can't remember the last time I ate in the dining room.'

A smile lifted her cheeks. It was a smile that could stop traffic. It certainly stopped his heart from beating effectively. 'You eat like a native New Yorker.'

'How do you know what a native New Yorker eats?'

'I've been getting tips from Marcy.'

His laughter came as automatically as his body's raging war. 'Now, she *is* a native New Yorker.'

Ciro swallowed his first mouthful of Chicken Cacciatore and stared at the woman who'd made it.

Her fork, halfway to her delectable mouth, hovered mid-air. 'Is it okay?'

'Claudia, this is fantastic.'

Her cheeks stained pink, her pleasure at his compliment obvious.

'I know you like to cook but this is something else—this is restaurant standard.'

Now the staining on her cheeks was of embarrassment. 'Don't be silly.'

'I'm serious. And I say it as someone who's dined in many Michelin-starred restaurants.'

Her furrowed brow showed her continued scepticism but instead of arguing, she popped a forkful of chicken into her mouth.

He had a sip of the wine she'd opened and found it complemented the dish perfectly. 'Who recommended the wine?'

The furrow on her brow deepened. 'It's the wine I always serve with this dish.'

'Are you a secret sommelier?'

'What's a sommelier?'

'A professional wine steward. They're trained to pair food with wine.'

'People are *paid* to do that?' She pulled a musing face. 'As our English nanny used to say, you learn something new every day. Whenever I used to make a new dish I would raid Papà's wine cellar until I found the perfect wine to go with it.'

Ciro fought not to let the clenching of his guts at the mention of her father show on his face. Claudia was making a huge sacrifice to allow him to be father to their child. She must hate him for what he'd done to her but she was putting their baby's needs above her own and he needed to do the same. Somehow he must learn to separate her from her father. If he couldn't, then how could he separate his child from its grandfather?

He'd come to think her insistence on living with him until the birth was the right call.

'Trial and error?' he asked.

She nodded, then gave a sudden giggle. It was so rare and unexpected that it sounded like music to his ears. 'Once, when I was trying out a new Tuscan recipe, I sampled eight bottles of red. He wasn't very happy with me—one of them was a ten-thousand-euro Barolo.'

'Did it pair with the recipe?'

Her initial giggle turned into a peal of laughter. 'No!'

'You clearly have a good nose.'

Shoulders shaking with mirth, she twitched said nose. It was such a ridiculous gesture that Ciro found himself laughing too. He drank some more of the superb wine then looked at Claudia's glass of water. His good humour wilted. She was drinking water rather than wine, he guessed, because she'd sworn off alcohol for the pregnancy. She'd never struck him as much of a drinker, but, like the majority of their compatriots, was partial to a glass of wine with her evening meal.

Claudia must have sensed a dimming in his mood. 'What's wrong?'

He met the dark brown stare that seemed to

read him so easily. 'I'm just thinking how easy men have pregnancy.'

She leaned across the table to pat his hand, her eyes mock-rueful. 'You wait until I'm the size of a whale and craving toothpaste on toast. You won't find it so easy then, having to run around after me.'

It took a moment for her jocular words to penetrate because at the first touch of her skin on his, a jolt of sensation dived through his bloodstream. Claudia must have made her tactile display without thinking for her cheeks suddenly coloured and she quickly removed it, leaving an imprint on the top of his hand so warm it should glow red.

The pads of Claudia's fingers tingled madly, the nerves begging her to reach out and touch him again. She gripped her glass of water tightly and tried to pretend nothing had happened, pretend to be calm but, really, what had she been *thinking*?

She hadn't been thinking. She'd been enjoying the moment and the lowering of their respective barriers and, for a few seconds, had forgotten herself and slipped into an intimacy neither of them wanted.

But…

The butterflies had started off again. In truth, they hadn't shut up since he'd walked into the library. Everything inside her just felt so much more alive when Ciro was around, her senses heightened so much she could feel the drumbeats of her heart and hear the blood whooshing in her veins.

When she dared look at him again, his jawline was as tight as his smile. 'I know very little about pregnancy,' he said, clearly going down the *let's-pretend-that-never-happened* route. 'I'm aware of the physical changes it brings but the rest of it…' He shrugged. 'I know you're going to need my support but you'll have to tell me when you need it because I'm clueless.'

'I don't know much more than you,' she admitted. 'Once we've seen a doctor everything should be clearer.'

'You want me to come with you?'

'You're the father. You should be there.'

'I don't have to travel anywhere next week so I'll get an appointment made for a day then. Does that work for you?'

'My diary's a little full but I'm sure I can rearrange things to fit it in.'

Their eyes held. Her heart skipped to see amusement spark in his stare. And something else. Something that took hold of her skipping heart and squeezed it tightly before releasing it to send blood exploding through her.

* * *

Claudia stood in front of the mirror in her dressing room and brushed her hair. She'd had a shower, brushed her teeth and changed into her pyjamas, her usual bedtime routine, but there was nothing usual about how she was feeling. Her stomach churned with such strength she wished she could put it down to pregnancy nausea. But she couldn't. She'd fooled herself before about her feelings, insisting to herself and her sister that she did love Ciro when all along it had been deep attraction mingled with a plaintive need for the freedom he represented. She wouldn't lie to herself again.

But her attraction to Ciro hadn't died. It still burned inside her. There had been a moment towards the end of their meal when their eyes had locked again and she'd suddenly been consumed with memories of the feelings and sensations that had erupted in her when they'd made love. She felt them on her skin now. And inside her too. Ripples of heat low in her pelvis, a hungry ache…

Gritting her teeth, she began plaiting her hair as she always did before bed.

How could she still feel such physical hunger for him? Ciro had played her for a fool in a sick game of revenge. She'd swallowed his lies about love and while she accepted her words of love had been a lie too, she'd never meant to be deceitful. He *had* meant to be deceitful. If she hadn't overheard him, she would still be ignorant of the game he'd been playing. Imma was convinced the Trapani brothers' ultimate aim had been the entire Buscetta family's destruction.

Claudia wanted them to build a supportive relationship for their baby's sake but she would never trust him again.

'We need to get you a dressing table.'

She gave a small scream. So lost had she been in her thoughts she hadn't heard Ciro enter the bedroom. 'You startled me!'

When their meal had finished the semi-easy atmosphere between them had suddenly changed. Conversation had become stilted. Eye contact had ceased. And the charge in her veins...

She'd got up from the table abruptly, frightened of all the feelings rampaging through her. 'I'm going to bed now.'

He'd still had half a glass of wine to drink. He'd looked at her briefly before swirling the dark liquid and giving a short nod. 'Sleep well.'

She hadn't asked if he'd be joining her in the bed. She hadn't known which answer she most wanted to hear.

This was the first time he'd entered the bedroom with her in it since her first morning.

She met his eyes in the reflection of the mirror. A faint smile tugged on his cheeks. 'I'll call out next time.'

Breaking the eye contact, she continued working on the French plait and pretended not to notice Ciro watching her from the dressing room's threshold. She couldn't pretend the butterflies weren't flapping and dancing in her belly or that her usually steady hands didn't have a tremor in them.

Ciro knew he needed to move. The longer he stood watching Claudia plait her beautiful hair, the stronger his yearning to stand behind her and unplait it as he'd done on their wedding night and run his fingers through those silky strands. The stronger his arousal.

When she'd finished the plait, she used a band she'd had wrapped around her wrist to secure it. Her eyes found his again.

He inhaled deeply through his nose. 'I'm going to brush my teeth.'

She answered with a nod but didn't move.

Forcing his body to co-operate with his brain, he performed an abrupt turn and walked to the en suite. Before he stepped in his senses were assailed with the scent of Claudia's shower gel and the mintiness of her toothpaste. His chest closed so tightly he could hardly breathe. He opened the bathroom cabinet, saw her toothpaste and toothbrush in a glass together on the top shelf, and almost smiled to remember her quip about craving toothpaste on toast.

Ciro had personally designed his bathroom. Not once in the planning had he imagined he would one day walk into it and see a woman's toiletries neatly arranged in his cabinet and feel that his heart could pound out of his chest. The cabinet had four shelves. Claudia hadn't moved any of his stuff, her own carefully placed so as not to intrude.

Placing his hands knuckles-down on the sink, he took some more deep breaths. He *must* get a handle on this. He'd decided on the flight back to New York that he couldn't sleep on the library sofa again. He'd torn a muscle in his back a few years ago, one of those injuries that could easily recur without warning. Two nights on a sofa followed by two nights on his firm LA bed had reminded him of the importance of sleeping on a decent mattress.

Claudia was going to live with him for the foreseeable future. He'd agreed they would share a room for a few weeks and it was time to bite the bullet and do it. He had no doubt he was in for some nights of torture but it wasn't for ever, only a few weeks, and then she'd move into a guest room far away from him.

Face washed and teeth brushed, he stripped

down to his boxer shorts. No more sleeping nude for him. He'd always assumed he'd have retired before he started thinking about wearing pyjamas. Maybe it was time to bring those pyjama-related retirement plans forward.

Claudia had drawn the curtains and was curled up in bed when he left the en suite. Not until he climbed in beside her did she speak. 'You're sleeping with me?'

'Yes.' He turned the light out.

Plunged into darkness, they lay backs turned, the bed large enough for them both to stretch out without encroaching on the other's space.

The distance wasn't enough. There was not a single cell in his body not alert to Claudia's presence beside him. The thudding of his heart was deafening.

Claudia was afraid to breathe…no, she *couldn't* breathe. From the moment the mattress had made the slight dip to accommodate Ciro's hulking form, her lungs had closed. She was afraid to move. One small movement might find her brushing against him. She squeezed her eyes tightly shut, trying to block out the tingling warmth growing low in her pelvis. She still couldn't breathe. She couldn't hear Ciro breathe either. They both lay with the rigid stillness of one of his statues. They could *be* a couple of statues, lying there as a form of modern art.

Her left arm, tucked at an awkward angle under her pillow, started to ache. But she didn't dare move.

She felt her temperature rise, heating from the inside, the waves flowing to her skin. The four nights she'd already spent in this bed had been without any issue whatsoever. Ciro kept his apartment at a Goldilocks temperature, which she'd found, until this moment, to be just right. The mattress was firm and comfortable, the duvet soft yet heavy, the two cocooning her to sleep as if they'd been designed with her needs in mind. She'd slept better in this bed than she'd ever slept before. But that was then.

Ciro kept as firmly to his side of the bed as she kept to hers. There had to be a foot of empty space between them but her whole body was as hot as if he'd draped himself over her. Her heart thrummed as madly as when he'd kissed her.

Eventually, she could bear it no longer and slowly poked her foot out from under the duvet. It brought a welcome coolness to her foot but the rest of her still burned and her awkwardly placed arm was now killing her. With a burst of impetus, she shoved the duvet off and rolled onto her back. She didn't know which was the greatest relief: the chilly air on her skin or the blood flowing through her left arm and shoulder.

Ciro shifted beside her.

She held her breath. She was quite certain he was still awake.

Awake or not, he didn't make any further movements, not in all the time it took for her to eventually drift into sleep.

CHAPTER NINE

CIRO SLIPPED OUT of bed, slung a pair of shorts on and headed straight to his gym. He needed to work these awful, conflicting, heady feelings out of his system.

He'd woken with an erection to rival the Empire State Building and had been on the verge of waking Claudia with a kiss to the nape of her neck before sanity had washed through the last of his sleepiness.

He'd never known torture like that existed. To lie beside Claudia and not touch her had been as close to hell as he'd ever experienced.

He wished he had the power to accelerate time to the birth of their child. He'd buy her an apartment close enough that he could have easy contact with the baby but far enough away that he wouldn't run the risk of bumping into Claudia.

That day couldn't come soon enough. She hadn't even been here a week and already he could feel himself unravelling at the seams.

* * *

Claudia didn't think she'd had a worse night's sleep in her life. The only mercy came when she woke to find Ciro already up and gone. She showered and dressed quickly then wandered to the kitchen to make herself a hot chocolate. She was sipping it on the terrace when he finally appeared, dressed in a black T-shirt and faded jeans and carrying a mug of coffee. She had no idea where in the apartment he'd been hiding.

She tightened her hold on the mug and hoped his eyesight wasn't good enough to see the sudden clatter of her heartbeat.

His eyesight could have been the best in the world and he wouldn't have noticed. He took the seat furthest from her, nodded a tight-lipped greeting without meeting her eye, and swiped his phone on.

'Have you got laryngitis?' she asked after a few minutes of being ignored.

He raised narrowed eyes. 'Why do you ask that?'

'Because you haven't said a word since you joined me. I thought things went pretty well between us over dinner last night but here we are now and you're sitting there ignoring me again. You blow hot and cold…it's hard,' she finished with a shrug.

He put his phone down. So many differing

emotions flared in the green of his eyes that, for once, it was difficult to judge what he was thinking. A pulse throbbed on his temple. When he spoke his rich voice was curt. 'I don't know how to be around you.'

'Just be yourself. Isn't that the whole point of this? For us to be honest about who we are? For us to try and forge something that will allow us to be parents together?'

The pulse on his temple seemed to go haywire. 'I'm trying but it's harder than I thought it would be. Much harder. I look at you and see this beautiful, innocent woman who I've treated appallingly and then I remember you're the daughter of the man who killed my father. My heart tells me you were ignorant of his criminal ways, but my head can't see how you lived with someone your entire life and remained blind to his true nature. Forget your dyslexia, you're a smart woman and you're observant. You notice *everything*. So tell me how I'm supposed to believe you were ignorant to who your father really was.'

No one had ever called her smart before but she couldn't savour this unexpected compliment because too many other emotions were swelling inside her.

'There was no one there to contradict him.' Agitated, she put her mug on the table and gathered her hair together. 'I wish I could make you see what it was like for us growing up. I was three when Mamma died. I don't remember anything before that and I don't know if her death made Papà more protective than he would have been.' As she plaited her hair, Claudia wished with all her heart that her sister could be there with her. She missed her badly. Imma would know the right words to say. 'I never had any freedom. Whenever we left the villa it was always with armed guards protecting us, even at school—and our school was probably the smallest and safest in the whole of Sicily. I was never allowed to go to friends' homes like the other girls were. I never mixed with boys. The only people we mixed with were paid by my father. They weren't going to tell us the truth, were they?'

'But you must have known there was something crooked about him. You believed me when I told you what he'd done to my father. If someone had told me something like that about my father I would have laughed in their face because he was a good, honest man with scruples. You believed it without question.'

'It was…' She thought frantically for the right way to explain it. 'I wasn't completely blind. I always knew there was a darkness to Papà and it's something that's scared me since I was a little girl. It's partly what made me so obedient.

When you told me what he'd done…something clicked into place. Things I'd been too afraid to talk about, feelings I'd had, things I'd seen and heard that made no sense, the fear that's always lived in me… Like a giant jigsaw puzzle with all the pieces suddenly slotting together. I knew in my heart you were telling the truth. One of the reasons I went to the convent when I left you was because those nuns educated me. They've known me since I was six. Many of them educated my mother. I learned things from them that made other things click into place too.'

'What things?'

'Like my dyslexia. Like the whole of Sicily being frightened of him. That it's not just your family he terrorised. That the home I grew up in comes from money that's been paid for by other people's blood. For you to think I'd be complicit in any of that…' She blinked back hot tears. 'Whatever happens between you and me, I will never go back to him. I'd rather live on the streets.'

Her plait done, she went to pull the band off her wrist to tie it together but her wrist was bare.

For the longest time the only sound was the heaviness of Ciro's breaths. His frame was stiff, his features rigid, his green eyes intent on her face.

And then, slowly, his shoulders loosened and the expression in his eyes softened.

'I'm sorry.' He gave a laugh that sounded rueful rather than humorous. 'I keep having to apologise, don't I?'

She thought of what her father had done to his family and a fresh burn of tears set off behind her eyes. She swallowed them away and croaked, 'This isn't easy for either of us.'

His Adam's apple moved. 'I'm making it harder than it should be. I'll try harder. I promise.'

Their gazes lingered before he drained his coffee. 'I promised to show you around the city. Is there anywhere in particular you'd like to go?'

Relief blew through her veins at the change of subject. Much more of it and she wouldn't have been able to hold the tears back any longer. She didn't want to cry in front of Ciro. She pointed at the sprawling canopy of trees and cleared her throat. 'I'd like to go there.'

'Central Park?'

'*That's* Central Park?' Old childhood movies flashed in her mind. 'Don't they do horse and carriage rides there?'

'They do. Would you like to go on one?'

A sliver of excitement unfurled in her. 'I'd love to.'

'Anything else?'

'I keep thinking I see a castle…'

'That's Belvedere Castle.'

'Can we go there too?'

'We can go anywhere you like.'

Ciro left the elevator and expelled the air he'd been holding the whole way down. Every time he inhaled Claudia's scent his senses ran riot and his fingers itched to touch her. He was grimly determined that however their weekend panned out, he would be cordial and engaging. He hadn't meant to be cruel and ignore her earlier but when he'd walked onto the terrace, the urge to haul her into his arms had been so potent that he'd needed to drag his focus away from her until he'd regained control of himself.

None of this was Claudia's fault. She hadn't asked to be played in his game of vengeance. It wasn't her fault that she intoxicated him.

He had to accept that he'd got her wrong. Everything about her. All wrong.

And now he owed it to her and their baby to try. To really try. And that started now.

His vow almost shattered a moment later when they went to step outside the building to begin their sightseeing tour and Claudia suddenly grabbed hold of his hand.

The jolt of electricity that rushed through his veins was more powerful than when she'd patted his hand over dinner, but her hold was too tight to shake off.

'Look at all the *people*,' she breathed, eyes wide.

Feeling the fear vibrate through her, and seeing the golden colour of her skin turn ashen, he felt a wave of something like compassion join the electrical rush. And anger.

Cesare had done this to her with his horror stories.

He'd never believed his loathing of the man could increase but in that moment it did.

Relaxing his clenched jaw, he forced a smile to his lips. 'You have nothing to be frightened of. These people are just going about their business, the same as we are.'

'What if I lose you?'

'I'll stick to you like glue.'

She kept her eyes on his for the longest time before taking a deep breath. Dropping his hand, Claudia lifted her chin and stepped onto the bustling street. There was a bravery to her movements that made his heart twist unbearably.

Ciro stepped into the apartment at the same moment Claudia reached the bottom of the stairs. She was still in her pyjamas. Judging by the puffiness of her eyes, she'd only recently woken.

'Good timing,' he said, holding up the paper

bag in his hand. 'Breakfast. Shall we eat on the terrace?'

She gave a wide yawn and blinked vigorously, then followed it with a smile.

He walked behind her up the two flights of stairs to the bedroom and through the French doors. Her bottom was only inches from his eyeline...

Claudia, he suddenly realised, had the peachiest bottom in the world. As she normally wore long, loose-fitting tops over slim jeans or trousers, her bottom was usually hidden, but the silk of her pyjamas accentuated its peachiness. It took real effort not to let his gaze lock on it.

'What have we got?' she asked as she sat on the wrought-iron chair with its soft cushion to pad her bottom.

Damn, he was thinking about her bottom. Again.

But how had he not noticed its divine peachiness before?

'Bagels.' He opened the bag and removed the contents. 'This one is egg, cheese and bacon.' He pulled the second bagel out. 'This is avocado, bacon and cream cheese. Take your pick.'

She smiled, enthusiasm and gratitude flashing in her eyes. 'These smell delicious. I've never had a bagel before.'

He popped the lip of his coffee lid then remembered the carton in his pocket. 'I got you peach juice.' The one real pregnancy symptom Claudia was suffering was her stomach recoiling from coffee.

'*Peach* juice? Is that a thing?'

'Orange juice,' he corrected, silently cursing himself for his slip of the tongue. 'I meant orange juice. Please, take your pick of the bagels.'

'Which one do you want?'

'Stop being polite and take one.' She went for the avocado. Her lips parted and she took a generous bite. As she chewed, her eyes met his, beaming her pleasure at him.

Arousal, which he'd been fighting since following her up the stairs, broke free and shot through him like a heated blade.

Damn, damn, damn.

Mercifully, the table hid the discomfort he was experiencing in his trousers. Thank God he'd be leaving for the office soon and could put some distance between them. He needed it. Three nights spent trying to sleep beside Claudia coupled with two days showing her around their immediate neighbourhood and some of the sights New York had to offer had done nothing to dent his awareness. Familiarity had not lessened his attraction to her one iota. The opposite had occurred. Saturday night had been worse than Friday, the image of her delighted face when they'd taken the horse and carriage ride a continual flash behind his retinas.

Yesterday, Sunday, he'd been determined to exhaust himself enough that he crashed out the moment his head hit the pillow. They'd walked for miles, followed by a long evening watching a Broadway show. He'd still hit his pillow with energy to burn. He'd still lain on his bed with heat raging through his loins and every one of his senses attuned to the woman sleeping with her back to him.

He watched her fold her wrapper into a neat square before placing it back in the paper bag.

He wanted to reach out and pull her to him. He wanted that peachy bottom on his lap and grinding into his arousal...

He finished his bagel with one large bite and pushed his chair back. 'I should get to work.'

Claudia could hardly comprehend the wrench she felt at this.

The weekend they'd shared had gone much better than she'd hoped. Clearing the air of her bottled-up feelings had definitely helped and she vowed never to hold back from speaking her mind again.

They'd walked for miles and talked for hours. Who would have thought they'd share a love for old Hollywood movies? Who'd have believed their top ten movies shared seven in common?

But what had really touched her was the way Ciro had accommodated her dyslexia without being asked and without it even being mentioned. At the American Museum of Natural History, he'd read the exhibit descriptors to her just as he now read menus to her and all without making it obvious and heaping embarrassment on her. He simply took it in his stride and not once did he patronise her.

And now he was going to work and the weekend they'd shared would be officially over.

It scared her how badly she wished he would stay.

She shouldn't feel like this. One nice weekend with this man didn't change what he'd done to her or alter the fact that she couldn't trust him. She was only here for their baby. He only let her be here for the baby.

But still she wished he would stay.

'Of course,' she said steadily. 'And I should shower. I hope your day goes well.'

The violence in her stomach was as frightening as her wayward thoughts and, terrified she really would ask him to stay, she got hurriedly to her feet but, in her haste, her thigh bashed against the table. Before she had time to register what was happening, Ciro's barely touched coffee toppled over. The lid flipped off and hot black liquid gushed over the table and spilled onto his lap.

Horror spilled through her as quickly as the coffee had spilled. 'Oh, God, Ciro, I'm *sorry*,' she cried, hurrying over to him. 'Are you hurt?'

He looked more disbelieving than pained. His gaze drifted to his lap. The coffee had spilt over his left thigh and soaked through the fabric of his charcoal trousers. There were splatters of black coffee on his white shirt too.

Guilt and panic set in. 'You need to take those off.'

He held a hand up to her, an unspoken warning to keep back. 'I'm not hurt.'

Getting to his feet, he strolled into the bedroom and disappeared into the en suite, closing the door behind him.

Claudia hovered outside the door, wringing her hands together. When she couldn't stand the wait any longer, she knocked on it. 'Ciro? Are you okay? Is there anything I can do?'

More long minutes passed before the door opened. Ciro had stripped his clothes off down to his snug black boxer shorts. She looked down to his thighs and was horrified to see the left one marked a bright, angry red.

Covering her mouth, she burst into tears. She'd never done anything to harm anyone before, not ever, and to see the damage she'd inflicted on

his thigh was more than she could bear. 'I'm…
so…sorry,' she gulped between sobbing breaths.

Now a pained look did cover his face. Through
the muffling of her ears, she heard him curse
and then found herself pulled against his chest,
his strong arms wrapping around her and holding her tightly to him.

'Don't cry. It was an accident,' he murmured
into her hair.

Trying desperately to control her tears, Claudia tried even harder not to sink into him. Being
held like this, Ciro's warm breath brushing
through her hair, her cheek pressed against his
smooth chest, his heartbeat strong against her
ear, breathing in his woody scent…it all just felt
so *right*.

But, much as she wanted to stay right where
she was, Ciro was injured and she reluctantly
pulled out of his hold and gazed up at him. 'We
need to get you to hospital.'

He smoothed her hair from her face. There
was a tenderness to the gesture that made her
want to cry harder. 'I messaged my doctor a few
minutes ago. He'll be here shortly. I'm supposed
to run cold water over the injury while I wait
for him.'

'Then what are you doing comforting me?'
Snatching hold of his hand, she led him back
into the bathroom. 'Get in the bath.'

A wry smile played on his lips as he obeyed her bossy command, a smile that turned into a wince when he lifted his left leg in.

'How can you say it doesn't hurt?' Her heart hurt even more to see his obvious pain. She took the shower head off its attachment and turned the cold tap on.

'It didn't…' His eyes widened as she aimed the shower head on his injury. 'That's *cold*.'

She wiped the last of her tears away with the back of her free hand and attempted a smile. 'It's supposed to be.'

Ciro gritted his teeth against the pain, rested his head back and closed his eyes. He knew from experience that concentrating on the pain only made it worse. 'Talk to me.'

'About what?'

'Anything.' From feeling no pain, his thigh now felt as if someone had taken a blowtorch to it. 'Distract me. What did you dream of being when you were a little girl?'

'Working in a pastry shop.'

He opened one eye, about to query this unexpected answer. His attention was immediately taken by sight of her pyjama top. The spray from the showerhead had soaked into it. The white pyjama top had become translucent. Claudia's cherry-red nipples jutted out in all their erotic glory mere inches from his face.

Oblivious, she elaborated. 'Our nanny used to take us to a pastry shop every Saturday for a treat. We were allowed to choose one item and it could be whatever we wanted. I could never make my mind up because I wanted everything.'

He managed a pained laugh and dragged his gaze from her breasts to her eyes. Her eyes were every bit as beautiful as her breasts.

Still holding the spray on his thigh, she smiled, showing her small, pretty white teeth. 'What did *you* want to be?'

'A world-famous wrestler.'

Her peal of laughter cut through his pain like balm. 'And when did you decide that conquering the business world was better than being a wrestler?'

'When Papà told me it was all choreographed.' He shook his head in mock-sadness. 'He destroyed my dreams.'

'Liar.' She lifted the showerhead and aimed it at his chest, making him shudder at the unexpected blast of wet cold. Her grin widened at his reaction before she aimed it back on his injury.

'You have an evil streak in you.'

'So I'm learning.'

Their eyes locked together and, without any warning, Ciro found himself trapped in the molten depths of Claudia's beguiling eyes. Her smile dropped in a mirror image of his own disintegrating smile as a powerful charge surged between them. It happened so quickly he was powerless to stop it, powerless to stop the wave of unfiltered desire that crashed through him.

He wanted this woman more than he'd wanted anyone or anything in his life. Torture did not begin to describe how it felt to lie beside her night after night and not be able to touch her.

Why couldn't he touch her? In that moment, all his reasoning had flown out of the window. Every cell in his body vibrated in awareness of this ravishing woman. And, for the first time since their wedding night, he felt her body's vibrations of awareness of him too. It was there in the sudden shallowness of her breaths, in the heated swirling in her eyes, in the way she leaned closer to him…just as he leaned closer to her. The charge bound them both. He ached to touch her. To kiss her. To devour her. To mark her as his for ever…

Their faces had drawn so close together that he was inches from claiming those generous lips for his own when the intercom buzzed.

Claudia's eyes widened and she reared back. The showerhead slipped from her fingers and the cold water sprayed over his groin. The erection he hadn't noticed form—there had been too many other heightened sensations coursing through him to be aware of something as trivial as an erection—immediately deflated in protest at the frigid spray.

'That will be the doctor,' he managed to say as he grabbed the showerhead and saved his groin from frostbite. His words sounded faint inside the drumming of his head. 'If you press the top intercom button it will open the door for him.'

She blinked and nodded with equal rapidity, no longer looking at him. Her cheeks had turned the colour of tomatoes. 'I'll show him the way up.'

She was halfway out of the door moving at a speed that would have made a short-distance runner proud when he called after her. 'Claudia?'

She waited a beat before turning back to face him.

'You might want to change before you greet the doctor.'

She followed his gaze down to her chest. Immediately, she slapped an arm over her breasts. He didn't think there was a colour on the spectrum that could describe the colour cloaking her embarrassment.

CHAPTER TEN

'CAN I GET you anything else before I go to bed?'

Ciro's chest expanded at the melodious sound of Claudia's voice. He looked up from his book to see her enter the living room carrying two mugs of steaming hot chocolate, and found it expanding even more. 'I'm good, thank you.'

'You're sure?'

'I'm sure.'

Since the doctor left, Claudia had fussed around him like a mother hen. Her guilt at his burn—only minor, the damage only on the surface of the skin—was obvious but he had a strong feeling she would have looked after him even if she didn't feel responsible for it. As much as he'd always believed anyone with Buscetta blood's heart was stone, this day had proven as nothing else could that Claudia's heart was as soft as her skin.

Ciro's need for space away from her had been thwarted and they'd spent a whole day and evening together alone, trapped in the apartment. The torture of his nights had spilled over to his day and there had been no relief.

Whether Claudia had been whipping up delights in the kitchen or keeping him company in the living room watching an old movie they'd both loved as kids, he'd never been so aware of another human's presence. The gentle sway of her walk, the sound of her footsteps, the way she used her hands as an additional expression of speech, the way she pulled her knees to her chest and crossed her ankles when resting on the sofa… Every movement she made, every word she spoke, every breath she took, all soaked through his senses.

For once she wore something other than jeans or pyjamas, having matched one of her preferred loose tops with a short black skirt. Not only did she have the peachiest bottom in the world, but the shapeliest legs to match it.

With a shy smile, she put one of the mugs on the small table beside the reclining leather armchair he'd stretched out on, then drifted past him to stand at one of the living-room windows, cradling her own drink.

There was a long pause of silence while she gazed down at the bustling street storeys below. 'What made you move to New York?'

'New York's an old obsession of mine from

when I was a kid. Vicenzu came to university here, I visited, fell in love with it for real and followed in his footsteps.'

'But it's so big and so *busy*.' She sighed. 'Every time I step outside I think I'm going to get swallowed up. How do you get used to it?'

He put his book down and reached for his drink. 'I remember the moment I got out of the cab on my first visit here. I felt like a kid seeing Santa. I never had to get used to it because right from that moment, I knew I was exactly where I wanted to be.'

'Do you ever miss home?'

Home, he knew, meant Sicily.

He stretched his neck. 'Sometimes. When I hear a song my *mamma* likes or catch a movie I watched with my father.'

She looked at him and bit into her bottom lip. 'How is your *mamma* doing?'

He gave a heavy shrug and cleared his throat. 'She takes things a day at a time.'

Her eyes closed as if she were saying a silent prayer. 'Has it helped her, being back in her own home?'

Ciro didn't know how to explain things without hurting her. But with Claudia, only the truth would do. 'She doesn't want to live in it without my father.'

Her eyes widened and immediately filled with tears.

'Their marriage…it was solid, you know?'

She shook her head and he remembered she'd grown up without a mother.

'They loved us, me and Vicenzu, but they adored each other. When I was a teenager I would work with Papà in the school holidays… he always hoped one of us would take the business on…and I remember going into his office. I must have been fifteen, and he was chatting with his lawyer explaining why he didn't want to merge with an American conglomerate. He'd already turned down their offer of a buy-out. I think he'd accepted by then neither Vicenzu or I would take the business on but he hoped grandkids would come along and one of them would want it. But he turned down the big bucks for the buy-out and then he turned down the offer of a merger even though it would have given him financial stability. The olive industry can be precarious because you're at the mercy of the weather. One bad summer and the crop's ruined. He turned the merger down because it would have meant frequent travelling to America. He had a picture of Mamma on his lap and I *knew* he was turning it down because he couldn't bear to be parted from her. Mamma hates travelling.

She'll fly to Florence to visit her sister and that's enough for her.'

'Are you close to her?'

'Not as close as I should be,' he admitted. 'And it's entirely my fault. I couldn't wait to get out of Sicily. It was nothing against my parents, I just had this drive to get out into the world and make my mark. It was always in me. I remember thinking when I overheard that conversation between Papà and his lawyer that he was a fool. How could he turn all that money down? It would have set him up for life. But that was teenage arrogance on my part. I'm happy travelling the world and building an empire. My parents were happy living a simple life. Don't get me wrong, we had money. We never went without. But it wasn't a great fortune.' And certainly hadn't been enough to protect the business against Cesare's sabotage. 'All they wanted was to be together and for their boys to be happy. That was enough for them.'

There was a sharp stabbing in his guts as he thought, for the first time, about what his father would say if he knew his son had married a woman in vengeance. His father's heart had been big and generous.

He would be ashamed of him.

For the first time, Ciro could admit that he was ashamed of himself.

His parents had raised him well. He'd had love. A lot of love. He'd had their time. He'd had security. He'd had everything a child could ask.

They had raised him to be better than this.

'Do you have any memories of your mother?' he asked, suddenly keen to turn the subject away from himself. Claudia's mother, he'd learned, had died of bacterial meningitis, a swift and deadly disease if not treated early.

She tilted her head, her face screwing with concentration. 'Her shoes. I remember she had a pair of bright red heels. I remember trying to walk in them. I was so little they swallowed my feet.'

He swore his heart tore a shred. 'That's all you remember?'

'I think I remember her perfume. Sometimes I'll smell someone's perfume and it makes me think of her.'

Ciro knew exactly what she meant. In the five weeks Claudia had hidden away in the convent he'd imagined he'd smelt her perfume numerous times.

'I went in a perfume shop a few years ago trying to find it,' she said. 'I spent hours in there, spraying them all. I wanted to find it so badly but none of them was quite right. None of them was The One.'

Another shred tore from his heart. 'Didn't you ask your father?'

'He said Mamma wore lots of different perfumes. Imma doesn't remember the name of it either.'

'She was eight when your mother died, wasn't she?'

She nodded. 'Sometimes I envy all the memories she has of her. Imma's five years older than me so had five extra years with her. She remembers everything about her, right down to the softness of her skin and the texture of her hair. All I have is a vague sense of her perfume and a clear memory of one pair of shoes.'

'No wonder you envy your sister.'

'No, I envy her memories. She has the memories but she also has the pain. I was too young for Mamma's death to affect me much, but Imma...' Her chest rose. 'She never got over it. Her childhood ended that day.'

And, he suspected, Claudia's childhood had changed dramatically from the one she would have had if her mother hadn't died. There had been no one to counter her father's dominance and remove the clips he'd put on his daughters' wings.

The ideas Ciro had had about her growing up as a pampered princess were nothing but his own preconceived prejudices, just as everything else about Claudia had turned out to be.

As if she'd followed the train of his thoughts, she said, 'What my father did to your parents...' Her voice broke. 'Ciro, I wish I could take it all back. I wish I'd never told Papà I wanted my own house. Every time I think of calling him, I remember what he did to your father and God alone knows who else and I feel *sick*. How can a man who does the things he does call himself a child of God? How can he sleep at night? I don't understand it. I don't think I want to understand it.'

'Listen to me.' He straightened in his seat and stared at her, making sure he had her full attention. 'You are not responsible for what your father did.'

'If I hadn't mentioned my wish for a home of my own...'

'Don't think like that. None of this was your fault.' And it made him queasier than the most violent of hangovers to remember how he'd held her equally culpable.

One solitary teardrop fell. 'You believe me?'

'Yes.' Claudia would never be party to anything that hurt another person. If he hadn't been full of such rage and carried such a thirst for vengeance, he would have recognised that the first time he met her.

He just wished he'd realised the truth before destroying her life. How he would live with the guilt, he did not know.

Throat moving hard, chin wobbling, she rubbed her eyes with the palms of her hands then blew out a long puff of air. 'You don't know what that means to me.'

He could see what it meant.

Their eyes locked. Familiar, dangerous emotion fisted inside him. Trapped with only Claudia, he'd found himself staring at her too many times with a thudding heart and arousal coiling in his loins...and caught her staring back at him too many times to deny any longer that something was happening between them.

Under the soft lighting, he saw the flush cover her face before she looked away and murmured, 'I should get to bed.'

The dangerous feelings raging through him grew as she walked softly to him. She leaned down to pick up his empty mug. The fabric from her top brushed against his arm. Her scent swirled in his senses and that was the moment his hand took control and decided this was not something he could fight any longer.

He caught her loose plait and gently closed his fingers around it.

Time became suspended in the moment it took for her to turn her face towards him. Her chest rose and fell in short, ragged bursts and when those beautiful doe-like eyes locked onto his…

He lost the ability to breathe.

Claudia found herself caught. Trapped. Not in Ciro's light hold of her plait but in the weight of emotions pulsing from his eyes.

Her chest tightened and squeezed the air from her lungs. He slowly dragged his fingers to the base of the plait then released it to brush his fingers up her spine to her shoulder. Thrills raced through her. Every nerve ending in her body tingled in heightened anticipation of what he would do next.

He cupped the nape of her neck and gently pulled her to him.

Her heart thumped too hard for any other sound to penetrate. The ache she carried for him became a pulse of need that throbbed and swelled deep inside her. Ciro's breath swirled lightly over her lips and she closed her eyes to savour the sensation and its chocolatey warmth.

Her concentration had been shot since that moment in the bathroom when she'd been certain he was going to kiss her. She'd cooked and baked manically but her mind kept drifting back to their wedding night, her body reawakening to the memories with a vengeance that kept her short of breath. Everything she'd done and said since their almost-kiss had been with a heated weight in her pelvis and a fizz in her veins. Every time their eyes locked she'd felt such need rip through her that she'd had to hold onto something to stop her weakened legs swaying.

The hand not cupping her neck flattened against her cheek. His ragged breaths grew hotter and hotter against her tingling mouth until the firmness of his lips pressed against hers and every cell in her body melted.

His kiss was slow. Incredibly slow. Sensuous. An exploration. An erotic fusion that sent dizzying thrills soaring through her. One hand massaged her neck, the other caressed her cheek before gliding down her arm and winding across her back.

He pulled back to gaze into her eyes. There was pain in the green depths but it was a pain she understood, a pain she shared. It was the pain of a desire grown so big it could no longer be contained. A groan vibrated through his powerful chest and with one effortless tug, he pulled her onto his lap and sealed their bodies together. And then he devoured her mouth with the hunger of a starving man.

Oh, but this kiss was *everything*.

Claudia had been raised to believe only men craved sex and that women endured it. Her attraction to Ciro had been instant, there right from the start, but she'd been too frightened of the act itself to imagine it with anything but a broad brush. She'd hungered for Ciro but not for sex… Not until she'd spent the most magical night of her life with him. Everything she'd discovered only hours later had shattered her innocence more than the deed itself, but the memories of that time with him had refused to die.

Ciro had ignited a fire in her belly. Attempts to dampen it had come to nothing. The long nights sharing a bed with him, aching for his touch, longing for the magic that had made her one and only time with him so incredible had made her hunger for him turn into its own life force. She craved him. She ached for his touch, yearned to experience the wonder of it again without fear and simply enjoy the incredible sensations he roused in her and the closeness they'd shared.

Chests fused together, their mouths moved at a ferocious tempo. Ciro's hands roved everywhere, sweeping over her back and down her sides, over her thighs, cupping her bottom and then moving back up to tug her hairband off and throw it to one side. His fingers worked quickly to undo the plait and then ran through her hair until it fell like a sheet over them both and he turned his face to inhale its scent.

Holding her securely, he lay back on the recliner, taking her with him until she was straddling him and their lips locked together again.

Claudia kissed him with all the passion contained in her soul and then she kissed his neck, marvelling at the strength of it, the woody scent and smoothness of his skin, before finding his mouth again and melting into more of their erotic lip-play. While their mouths and tongues danced their seductive duel, Ciro lifted her top up. Somehow she managed to free her arms without having to move her mouth from his but to get it over her head meant breaking the lock. She shifted her position so her weight wasn't on his burn… and immediately felt the hardness of his erection right there between her legs. The pulse that tore through her was so powerful that she had no control of the moan that flew from her mouth.

Dazed, she reared back to stare into his eyes again, needing to see as well as feel that these dizzying feelings weren't hers alone. It felt as if her heart could beat right out of her chest.

He reached an arm up to rub the backs of his fingers down her cheek, his voice hoarse as he said, 'What are you doing to me?'

She had no idea what he was talking about.

He must have understood her ignorance. He cupped her cheeks and pulled her down so the tips of their noses touched. 'I have never wanted anyone the way I want you.'

The potency of his words was thrillingly immediate. She kissed him. 'I've never wanted anyone. Only you.'

Ciro's heart swelled with the same force as the swelling in his loins. Never had he wanted to possess someone the way he wanted to possess Claudia. He didn't want to have sex with her. He didn't even want to make love to her. He wanted to be as one with her, something he didn't even pretend to try and understand, just knew in that moment that that was how he felt.

'Take your top off,' he said thickly, then found the rest of him thickening too when she whipped it over her head and threw it onto the floor.

Her plain white bra tugged at his heart. They'd made love once before but in many ways Claudia was still an innocent with no clue as to the power she held in her sensual body.

She had power over him. That much he knew for certain. If someone told him right then that to take possession of Claudia meant he lost everything else, he would lose it all gladly.

He unclasped the bra and her beautiful, generous breasts spilled free. Lifting his head, he took one nipple into his mouth and was gratified to hear her moan of pleasure. She ground onto him but there was no relief, only further torture. Never in his whole life had he needed to be inside someone the way he needed to be inside Claudia.

The same urgency was in her too. He could feel it in her every touch and kiss and in the way she scratched at his T-shirt. Arching his back, he helped her remove it and then tugged his shorts down to free his erection from its constraints. Her arms wound around his neck, their chests fused back together, and she ground down on him with even more urgency. 'Ciro, please. I want...' Her words died on her lips as another moan fell in their place.

He rubbed his hands over her back and down to her bottom. Slipping his hand under her skirt, he groaned as he clasped the peachiness.

Her face, flushed with passion, hovered over his, her breaths short gasps. 'Ciro. *Please.*'

The only barrier between them now was her knickers. With her pleas for possession ringing in his ears and the feeling that he could spontaneously combust at any moment he wound them as tightly as he could and then ripped them apart.

He didn't know if he thrust up or if Claudia ground down or if it was a combination of both but the second that last barrier between them was gone, he was inside her tight, wet confines and fighting harder than he had ever done before to stop an instant climax.

Gritting his teeth, he wrapped an arm around her waist and clasped her bottom with the other hand, then held on for dear life as she began to move in earnest. That she was moving on instinct only made it more potent.

Her moans grew loader as she rode him, mouth on his cheek, her breasts crushed against his chest. Ciro did everything he could to hold on but this was too much, the sensations ripping through him were just too much, he was clinging by his fingertips… But then the tone of her moans became a breathy pitch and he felt her thicken around his raging arousal. Wrapping his arms even more tightly around her, he thrust up one last time and, with a loud shout that roared from deep in his chest, let go.

Claudia, dazed and utterly spent, finally loosened her hold around Ciro's neck and nuzzled into the crook. His woody scent had a new musky hue to it and she sniffed it with a sigh and rested her hand on his shoulder, closing her eyes to the gentle but no less potent sensations penetrating her skin as he stroked her back. Their chests were bonded so tightly together she could feel his heart beating in tandem with her own.

'Is your thigh okay?' she murmured.

He pressed his mouth to the top of her head and strengthened his hold around her.

Slowly, she drifted to sleep, waking only when he shifted beneath her. She lifted her head and found him staring at her with a look that made her heart soar.

'Ready to go to bed now?' he asked, his voice husky, before he pulled her down for a long, lingering kiss.

That kiss, more even than the earth-shattering pleasure of his lovemaking, made her feel that her world had changed for ever.

CHAPTER ELEVEN

CLAUDIA CREPT THROUGH the darkness to her dressing room and donned the first items of clothing that came to hand before slipping out of the bedroom and calling her sister. She had a good excuse to call but what she really wanted— needed—was to hear Imma's voice.

A night of making love to Ciro had left her as confused and out-of-sorts as she'd ever been.

It had been wonderful. Magical. Heavenly.

And yet all she wanted was to curl herself into a ball and bawl her eyes out.

She was not supposed to sleep with him. That had never been part of their agreement.

But, sweet Lord, it had felt so right. At least it had until Ciro had fallen asleep and her chest had started to tighten around her thudding heart. The spacious walls of the apartment felt as if they were closing in on her.

Her feelings for him were veering danger-ously out of control. Somehow she had to find a way to lock them away because they could never have a future together as anything other than co-parents.

So she did the only thing she could when her feelings felt as if they might explode inside her. She baked.

Even before Ciro heard Claudia's voice, he knew she'd slipped out of bed. Only the faintest light filtered through the curtains. He squinted at his watch. Five a.m. He couldn't have been asleep for more than an hour. Yawning widely, he debated getting up, tracking her down and carrying her back to bed for another bout of lovemaking.

He'd never known a night like it.

But his exhaustion was such that when Ciro next opened his eyes he found he'd slept for another two hours. The bed was still empty.

He climbed out and got straight into the shower.

He lathered shampoo into his hair, the full weight of what he'd done to her sitting heavily in him. He'd stolen her innocence. He'd lied to her. Used her. Got her pregnant. And now they'd made love again.

Never had he had sex with a woman and felt as if the fabric holding him together were fraying at the seams. And now it had happened twice.

Both times with the same woman. And this time the fraying was a hundred times worse.

He'd just shared the best night of his life with the woman whose father's actions had directly caused his own father's great heart to collapse. He *knew* that was nothing to do with her; that she was as big a victim as anyone—maybe the biggest victim of all—but that didn't change the self-loathing that he could share such heady joy with his enemy's daughter.

He just could not reconcile the warring parts inside him.

Shower done, he had a quick shave, then threw a shirt and some trousers on.

As he walked down the second flight of stairs he was greeted with the unmistakable aroma of baking. His steps faltered as childhood memories of waking to similar scents hit him. His mother had often made fresh pastries to feed her growing boys and devoted husband.

How he wished he'd appreciated all they'd done for him more, wished he hadn't treated them as a twice-yearly obligation to be filled, always busy building his empire and experiencing life and assuming they would always be there.

He found Claudia washing her hands at the sink, wearing a knee-length emerald shirt dress, hair plaited, her legs and feet bare. She did not look like a woman who'd gone a whole night without sleep.

Her smile contained a touch of wariness, as did her murmured, 'Good morning.'

Desire pulsed through him, strong and relentless, pounding through his veins in that one meeting of their eyes, his thoughts immediately flying to the image of her naked in his arms.

Wrenching his stare from her guarded gaze, he ran his fingers through his hair to stop them reaching for her. 'I need to get to work.'

Her teeth razed her bottom lip, her next smile warier than the first. 'When will you be back?'

'I don't know. I've got three meetings scheduled and a conference call with Paris.'

'Would you like a bagel before you go?' She nodded at a tray of bagels lined up on a cooling rack on the worktop he'd failed to notice when he'd walked into the kitchen because his attention had been so thoroughly caught by her. That explained the evocative aroma.

'I'd better make it quick. My first meeting's in half an hour.'

'Smoked salmon and cream cheese?'

'Sounds great.'

While she pulled two plates out of the cupboard and got busy preparing breakfast for them, he remembered hearing her voice when he'd first woken briefly. 'Who were you talking to earlier?'

'Imma.'

'Is something wrong?'

She spread cream cheese over one half of each opened bagel. 'The voice activation app on my phone's stopped working. I needed a bagel recipe and I didn't want to wake you.'

'Did she read the recipe out to you?'

She nodded, layering the salmon above the cheese and then reaching for the black pepper grinder.

'How does that work if you can't write it down?'

'I remembered it. I can't read or write but I've taught myself to pay attention and retain information. Tell me a recipe once and I will remember it for ever. Read me a news article and I will remember it word for word.' She picked up one of the plates and handed it to him.

No wonder she'd been able to recall the words Ciro had said to his brother that fateful morning verbatim, he thought.

'Can you read *anything*?' he asked after he'd taken his first bite of what was easily the most delicious bagel he'd had in his life.

'My name, Imma's name, Papà and our surname. I struggle with Cesare but given enough time I can make it out.' A blush that went all the way to the roots of her hair covered her face. 'I can read your name too.'

That should *not* make his heart thump.

'How come you were only recently diagnosed? Surely a condition as severe as yours should have been picked up years ago?'

'I've not had a formal diagnosis,' she explained. 'I talked to Sister Maria when I stayed at the convent recently. She was my first teacher. She told me they—the nuns—suspected I was dyslexic when I was six. They told my father but he hit the roof at the suggestion his princess might have something wrong with her. They did their best to help me but were too scared of him to fight my corner.'

'But surely your father must have realised you needed help? He must have read your school reports. Hell, all he had to do was compare your work to your sister's.'

The first hint of bitterness flashed over her face. 'I've been thinking about this a lot and I think having a stupid daughter suited him. He never got the son he wanted so he made Imma his business heir—she got all the brains—and decided I was more suited for being a decorative pet around the house. It's not like I was going to go off and forge a career, was it? I mean, come on, Ciro, who's going to employ someone who can't read or write and struggles with numbers?'

'You have a problem with numbers too?'

'I can see them individually, although I get my twos and fives muddled up, but put two numbers together and I can't see them. When I was little I wanted to work in my favourite pastry shop but when I asked them once—I couldn't have been more than ten—they said it involved more than just baking. I would have to do things like work the tills and stocktakes and write orders down. All the things I can't do.'

The thump in his heart now echoed violently in his guts as he remembered accusing her of wilfully signing her section of the transferred deed into her name. What had he said? Something about how she should have noticed the pathetically low sale price of it? Claudia would remember the exact words he'd used.

How badly wrong could one person be about another?

Ciro looked into the dark brown eyes of the woman in whose belly his developing child lived and felt as wretched as he'd ever done. A pampered princess? She should have been so lucky. This was the woman whose mother had died when she was three, leaving her at the mercy of a narcissistic father who'd exploited her severe learning difficulties for his own advantage so she would be dependent on him for ever…or until she married a man her father deemed worthy enough to look after her.

And in that moment, Ciro realised Cesare Buscetta *did* love his daughter. Because with hindsight came perspective. It hadn't been only Ciro's billionaire status that had attracted him as a prospective son-in-law but the strong family ties he'd grown up with. Cesare had assumed that Ciro would be as protective over his wife as his father had been over his and would shower his wife with the same amount of love. Assumptions Ciro had fed.

Whether it had been narcissism that had stopped him getting help for her or not, Cesare's protectiveness was undeniable. He'd seen Claudia's need for independence but had judged her—wrongly in Ciro's opinion—as not being ready for it so had sought the perfect property for her, one in which she could have that elusive freedom while still being under his care and protection. The Trapani family home.

He was about to say this to her when his phone buzzed, breaking the moment.

It was Marcy, reminding him of the meeting he was supposed to be at. He swore under his breath.

'You need to go?' Claudia guessed.

He nodded. 'I'm sorry.' He didn't even know what he was sorry for. And he didn't know why the sadness in her eyes felt so unbearable.

'Don't be.' She mustered a small smile. 'Are your offices far from here?'

'I thought I'd told you.' But obviously he hadn't because she would have remembered. 'My main office is on the other side of the floor.' At her blank expression he elaborated. 'You know where Marcy's stationed? Do you remember seeing the other door?' Thinking of Marcy, he took one of the freshly baked bagels for her.

'To the left of her desk?' Claudia asked.

'That's my private entrance into the offices. All my admin staff work from it.'

'I didn't know that.'

'It makes things easier to oversee, everything being under one roof.'

'Why doesn't Marcy work in there with them?'

'She does sometimes but she has a noise sensitivity. Call me if you need anything, okay?'

She nodded.

Bowing his head, he walked swiftly out of the kitchen, suddenly desperate to get away from this beguiling woman who had finally made him understand his enemy.

He understood Cesare's protectiveness towards Claudia. Because he felt it too.

Three days later, Claudia stepped out of the elevator and walked purposefully to the exit.

She could do this. She *would* do this.

The doorman smiled politely and opened the door for her.

Immediately, her senses were engulfed. Waves of people bustled past in all directions; tourists and dog-walkers heading to and from Central Park, shoppers, workers hurrying to appointments... People going about their business. That was what Ciro had said.

For the third night in a row, they'd made love long into the night.

They were still to talk about this change to their relationship and for that she was glad. Her feelings were so confused that she wouldn't know what to say. All she knew was that when it came to Ciro, she was helpless to resist. He'd woken something in her that overruled her rational thoughts.

Alone in the day, she would try to harden herself and remind herself that living with him was only a temporary thing until the baby was born. Then he would come home and she would look at him and find herself melting before he'd even touched her.

He'd left for work before she'd woken that morning but she had a vague memory of a brush of lips against hers and a gentle caress of a hand over her hair. She'd climbed out of bed, her chest tight and the need to get out and feel the sun on her face running strongly inside her.

Their being lovers did not change her ultimate goal. Real, unfettered freedom. How could she find it if she was too scared to leave the apartment on her own? Would Elizabeth Bennet hide in the shadows and wait for a man to take her hand to cross the road? No, she would not.

But it wasn't Elizabeth Bennet she brought to mind when she took the deepest breath of her life and joined the throng. It was Ciro.

Ciro closed his eyes before entering his apartment. It was the same every time he returned from work. He had to brace himself.

'Claudia?' he called.

'I'm in the kitchen.'

He should have guessed. His kitchen had had more use since Claudia moved in than in all the years he'd lived here. Ciro did not cook. With take-out, restaurants and cafés in New York being plentiful and catering to all tastes, he saw no need to hire a chef. Whatever he fancied at whatever particular time could be provided with one swipe of his phone. His kitchen had been re-modelled with the rest of the apartment only because it would have been out of keeping if he'd left it. It was a space he would have converted into something else if it wouldn't have devalued the apartment.

His guts knotting, he followed the growing

scent of fresh baking and found her loading the dishwasher. It didn't matter how many times he told her he employed staff to clean everything, she still insisted on cleaning up after herself. On the kitchen's island stood one of the biggest cakes he'd seen outside a wedding and decorated so beautifully it could be considered a work of art.

But the cake was only a peripheral observation for his gaze locked straight onto Claudia. Her jeans and T-shirt were covered in flour. Some had found its way into her hair and a great splodge of pink icing sugar sat on her left cheek. His chest squeezed around his heart so tightly that for a moment he couldn't speak.

Tearing his gaze from her, he looked again at the cake. 'That is amazing. Did you make it?'

She smiled and nodded. 'It's for Marcy's daughter. It's her birthday. They're having a party for her.'

'Marcy asked you to make it?'

'We got talking the other day. She told me she loved the bagels I'd made—I didn't realise you'd given one of them to her—and when I told her how bored I was here and how I used to bake for the convent she asked if I'd like to make the cake.'

'You baked for the convent?'

'Cakes and pastries mostly. They'd sell them

and put the money raised towards their good causes.'

'You've never mentioned that before.'

'It wasn't a regular thing. Just something I would do once or twice a week.'

'You don't consider that regular?' Ciro rubbed his fingers into his skull, wondering how the investigators he'd sent to dig into her background had missed this fact about her. But then, he had to acknowledge, they'd failed to infiltrate Cesare's home. Give the man his due, he surrounded himself with flunkies who were loyal.

'I wanted to do it every day but I kept getting under Papà's chefs' feet. They rationed my use of the villa's kitchen.'

He stared some more at the cake. 'I know people who would pay a fortune for a cake like that.'

'I wish I knew how to turn it into a career. The only things I'm good at are cooking and gardening.'

'You want a career?'

'All I've ever wanted is to be independent. I know you're going to buy me an apartment when the baby's born and pay maintenance for it but I don't want you keeping *me*.'

This was the first time Claudia had mentioned moving out since they'd become lovers. Hearing it from her mouth like that and the nonchalance with which she said it…

It made every sinew of his body tighten.

'You're my wife and the mother of my child,' he said, somehow managing to keep his tone even. 'You're my responsibility. Both of you.'

She looked him square in the eye. From the tone of her voice when she answered, she was struggling to keep her voice even too. 'I'm not your responsibility. I don't want to be your responsibility. I've had enough of being answerable to men. I will never deny our child anything but when I leave here I want to earn my own money. It might sound silly to you but I want to pay for my own clothes and all the things that are mine alone.'

'That doesn't sound silly,' he said, speaking through the lump that had formed in his throat. 'And knowing your strengths is a good place to start. Would you like me to look for a tutor who specialises in adult dyslexics? Someone who can help you in that respect?'

'That's very kind but your days are busy enough.'

'I will make the time. It's good that you're looking to the future. You're too young to spend the rest of your life with nothing to occupy you but while you're living here, let me provide for you. You're carrying my child and I feel enough guilt without having more added to it. If there's anything I can do to help you career-wise or in any other way, tell me. I *want* to help.'

He *did* want to help.

But he could not fathom why the thought of her leaving, a thought that only weeks before he'd believed couldn't come soon enough, now felt crippling. By rights, the time had nearly come for Claudia to move into a guest room. That thought was even harder to contemplate.

Breathing deeply to counteract the strange weight of emotion filling him, he looked away from the beautiful brown eyes and found his gaze locking on a huge bouquet of flowers displayed on the window sill. 'Where did they come from?'

Her face went so red that for a moment he was convinced she had an admirer. Then a worse thought occurred to him and he stared at them as if they'd grown poisonous tentacles. 'Are they from your father?'

She must have caught the tone of his voice for her eyes narrowed. 'Would it be a problem if they were?'

'This is my home.' His guts had filled with nauseous violence. 'I don't want to share my private space with anything that comes from that man.'

Her eyes narrowed further still. 'Half of my DNA comes from him.'

And didn't he wish he could forget that half? 'The better half must come from your mother.'

Claudia squeezed her eyes tightly shut, hating that in Ciro's eyes she would always be tainted. What did this say for his future relationship with their innocent baby, who he rarely spoke of, not even an idle question about potential names? He'd gone with her to see the doctor but even there he'd shown barely a glimmer of interest.

His cruel comment about her DNA felt like a knife in her heart.

When she was certain she'd held the burn of tears at bay, she put the dishwasher tablet in the slot then turned around to face him. 'I bought the flowers. I thought the apartment needed cheering up.'

'You ordered them?'

She shook her head. 'I walked to the florist and bought them there.'

'You left the apartment on your own?'

'Yes.'

'That's wonderful.' He remembered how tightly she had clung to his hand when they'd first stepped outside and the way she'd stuck so closely to him wherever they had gone. This had been a massive thing for her and she had done it. Just how incredible was she? 'I'm proud of you.'

'Proud that it means I'm less of a burden to you?' she challenged, jutting her chin in the air.

'Don't worry—I'll be gone before you know it, and you can stop worrying about my father tainting your precious space.'

'Claudia... I never meant it like that.'

'Don't *lie* to me. Now please excuse me, I need to shower.'

With what could only be called dignity, she left the kitchen, leaving Ciro staring at her retreating figure. It took all of a minute before guilt snaked into him.

CHAPTER TWELVE

CLAUDIA WAS ALREADY in the shower when Ciro entered the bedroom. She'd locked the bathroom door so he had to wait impatiently for her to finish. When she came out, a large towel wrapped around her damp body, she took one look at him, scowled, and folded her arms across her chest.

With a muttered curse, he scooped her into his arms and, before she had time to protest, laid her flat on the bed.

His face hovering above hers, he gazed into the dark brown eyes still burning loathing at him…and blazing with the same fire that lived inside him. 'You are not a burden to me,' he bit out. 'Do you have any idea how incredible you are? I'm proud of you for everything, *bedda*, from the way you fight your fears to the way you've trained your brain to compensate for your dyslexia…that, to me, is incredible. And sexy.' And then he sealed his words with the kiss he'd ached to plant on her beautiful generous lips from the moment he'd walked into the kitchen. The fusion of their mouths together acted as balm to his soul.

'I hate your father, yes, and I hate every reminder of him,' he murmured in a gentler tone, brushing his mouth over her cheeks and finding his way to her neck. 'I despise him for what he did to my father but I despise him too for what he did to *you*. You're his daughter but you are entirely your own woman.' He pulled her towel apart and let his eyes feast on the body that grew in beauty by the hour. 'And I want you more than I have ever wanted anyone.'

She didn't say anything but her breaths had become shallow. When he looked back into her eyes, something reflected at him from the molten depths that made his heart expand to match his arousal.

'I will be the first to admit that I've made mistakes—huge mistakes—where you're concerned,' he continued, tracing his hands over her body, thrilling at the little jolts and quivers she gave in response. 'I'm not perfect. I'm human.' He took one of her hands and guided it to his arousal. 'Everything I feel for you is more than I have felt before.'

Her eyes widened. Her fingers squeezed around it.

'See?' he said roughly as he dipped his head

to capture a perfect nipple in his mouth. She moaned and writhed beneath him. 'This is what you do to me. You drive me crazy. You are all I think about, day and night. I imagine us in bed...' He captured the other nipple and ran his tongue around it. 'I imagine making love to you all the time.' Making his way down her belly, he continued his sensual verbal assault. 'I want to touch every inch of your flesh.' He reached the top of her pubis. He could smell her hot excitement and filled his lungs with it. 'I want to open you up like a flower and taste your hidden secrets.'

Her moan seemed to come from her very core.

Claudia knew where he was going and knew too that all she had to do was close her legs or say no and he would stop. Since they'd become lovers, she'd waited with breathless anticipation for him to try and kiss her there again, never knowing if it was relief or disappointment she felt when he didn't. Because, since that moment of horror on their wedding night when he'd first tried to kiss her there—the classic books she enjoyed certainly didn't contain love scenes with an intimacy like *that*—she'd often found her thoughts drifting to it, heat bubbling inside her, wondering...

How would it feel? Would there be pleasure

in it for her as there was when he touched her there? Would Ciro take pleasure from it?

And then she melted like chocolate fondue to realise he'd been waiting for her to be comfortable with him as a lover, had understood that sex and intimacy for a recent virgin was a big deal. He'd been taking things slowly with her because he *did* understand her. He'd been taking things slowly because he cared for her.

And, as all these thoughts ran through her head, his tongue pressed against the centre of her pleasure that sent a shock of electricity jolting through her.

His tongue? She'd expected a brief brush of his lips...

'Relax,' he murmured as he shifted into a more comfortable position and gently parted her thighs. He looked up to meet her stare. She caught a flash of dimples before he buried his face between her legs.

His tongue pressed gently but firmly against her swollen bud, doing something to her that felt... Oh, it felt wonderful. One hand glided over her belly and she caught hold of it and squeezed it tightly, then closed her eyes and submitted to the most delicious pleasure imaginable.

She didn't want it to end.

How could she have thought something that felt so *incredible* was dirty or sinful? How naïve she had been. Ciro had opened her body to him and he'd opened her mind with it.

Whatever happened in the future, she would never regret their becoming lovers. If this was all they had then she would treasure these feelings for ever.

Then, just as she thought she'd reached the peak of sensual intensity, everything exploded inside her. She cried out his name, rippling sensations crashing through her and sending her soaring higher than she'd ever been before.

There was no time to catch her breath for the moment the waves began to subside, Ciro moved and kissed his way quickly up her belly and her breasts to her mouth—it took a beat for her to realise the strange new taste on his tongue belonged to her—and as he kissed her he drove deep inside her with a strength that had her crying his name out again and again, until she didn't know where she ended and he began.

It was only when it was all over and she lay dazed in his arms that she realised she had no idea when he'd removed his clothes.

Ciro tried to hold onto the dream. Beside him, Claudia shifted and snuggled closer, her warm hand groping in the dark for his.

He'd dreamed of their child. A beautiful baby

girl who looked exactly as he imagined Claudia had looked as a baby.

In his dream he'd been lying on the sofa with his daughter bouncing on his lap. The love that had filled his heart during the dream...

He tried to breathe but his heart had expanded so much it had squashed his lungs.

Over a month later and, to Claudia's delight, Ciro announced they were going to a gala at a trendy art gallery. With firm instructions to get herself a cocktail dress, she explored the women's section of his department store with a fawning personal shopper hanging on her arm telling her everything she tried on looked perfect.

Knowing perfectly well the shopper was ingratiating herself with the boss's wife, Claudia hid her amusement and enjoyed the experience. She'd never shopped for clothes before without having to think about how her father would react to seeing her in them.

Ciro, she knew, wouldn't care what she wore. All the same, she wanted to make him proud.

Things between them had changed immeasurably. She was in no doubt of the sincerity of both his guilt and his desire for her. He'd even cut short a five-day trip to Paris to three days. Heat engulfed her every time she remembered how he'd walked into the apartment, locked eyes with her and, without uttering a word, scooped her up and carried her to the bedroom.

Neither of them had mentioned the original agreement that she share his bed for only a few weeks. It hadn't needed mentioning.

She didn't know if it was the intimacy of the act he'd performed on her that made her feel they'd reached a whole new level of closeness but she felt as if they were properly together, a team, a couple, partners. For the first time since the wedding, she looked to the future with hope in her heart.

Their baby was due in less than six months. It wouldn't be long before her body began properly changing. So far, her belly had developed a slight roundness but she'd been assured that would suddenly accelerate and she'd turn into a beached whale. If that made the passion between them dwindle to nothing then she'd cross that bridge when she came to it. She was confident that they'd forged a good enough friendship that when she moved into her own apartment, they could co-parent their baby as friends. If the passion between them still existed…they'd find a way to make it work, even while living under separate roofs.

She hoped they could make it work but refused to take it for granted. She'd gone into their marriage blind. Now she refused to close her eyes.

Ciro had broken her heart before. She would not give him the ammunition to break it again.

She was coming to learn, though, that at heart he was a decent, thoughtful man. Sometimes she overheard him on the phone to his *mamma*. His patience and kindness with her made Claudia's heart ache. The ache would grow to know it was her father who'd destroyed Ciro's *mamma*'s life.

Three weeks ago, he'd given her the numbers of three tutors who specialised in dyslexic adults. He'd inputted the details into her phone and then dropped the subject. No pressure.

The tutor who'd sounded the friendliest was coming to the apartment on Monday.

Ideas for a career were formulating in her mind too, a career she could do in her future home with the baby at her side.

She took an age getting ready for the gala and when she was done and paraded herself in front of Ciro, his eyes widened and he wolf-whistled. She practically preened! If she'd ever mastered whistling herself, she would have whistled him because he *oozed* masculinity, his black dinner jacket emphasising his divine physique.

The look they exchanged in that moment was red hot. If they'd been within hand's reach of each other, their glamorous outfits would have been ripped off in seconds.

So it was with joy in her heart that she arrived at the gala with her hand wrapped tightly in Ciro's.

The art gallery itself was nothing as Claudia had imagined. She remembered a trip to Florence as a child of twelve to the Uffizi. Huge frescoed ceilings, exquisite sculptures and vast oil canvases rang large in her memories. It had felt like stepping back in time to a distant age. This gallery rivalled the Uffizi for size but there the similarities ended. Everything here was white, the floors, the walls, the ceilings, everything apart from the art itself, which was as different from the Uffizi's exhibits as night was from day. These pieces were *modern*, Ciro informed her. All guests were expected to enjoy them before the gala proper started.

The problem, she quickly found, was that these creations needed explaining.

Not being able to read hadn't marred her enjoyment at the Uffizi because the art spoke for itself. Caravaggio's *Sacrifice of Isaac* and Gentileschi's *Judith Beheading Holofernes*—Imma had read the titles to her—had horrified Claudia with their violence but she'd known immediately what they meant and what they were portraying.

Here, she didn't have the faintest idea what the huge cube that was taller than Ciro was supposed to mean. Or the dangling six-foot sculpture of a wooden chair. Or what one of the rare canvases to occasionally line the walls was supposed to represent; all she saw were splatters of random colour.

But, judging by the earnest talk around her as their fellow guests consulted their guide books, these were *'works of art, darling'*.

'Do you actually like this stuff?' she whispered to Ciro when she was certain no one was listening. His apartment was filled with the type of artwork she adored and which, when she had a place of her own and if she had the money, she would buy for herself.

He grinned and dipped his mouth to her ear. 'Awful, aren't they?'

Claudia gave a bark of laughter, absurdly pleased that they were of the same mind on yet another thing, then found her laughter muffled by Ciro's lips crushing hers for a very short but *very* hungry kiss.

The anticipation of what would happen when they got back home later thrummed through her veins. Judging by the lusty stares she kept getting from Ciro and the possessive way he kept hold of her hand, he was counting down the minutes too.

An extremely eccentric-looking couple joined them, clutching guide books to their chests.

'Have you been in the Angelino room yet?' the man asked. He wore a bright purple and yellow checked crushed velvet suit and a neon green bow tie. Claudia was so taken with his outfit that she failed to hear his question.

'Yes, we've been in there,' Ciro said, gently squeezing Claudia's hand. If her eyes got any wider they would pop out.

'What did you think of the Gatsby piece?'

That would be the floating hat, Ciro remembered. An ordinary, cream, Panama hat suspended between the wall and ceiling by seemingly invisible means. He thought quickly and remembered an old quote he'd read in a book one time. 'Fantastic,' he said with a beam, 'is not the word.'

'Quite,' the man said with an approving nod before turning to Claudia. 'And what do you think, young lady, of the Shadow piece?'

'Is that the mannequin one?' she asked, her hold on Ciro's hand tightening reflexively. He'd read the titles of all the pieces to her.

'Well, hardly a mannequin, but yes, that's the gist of it.'

How he would love to turn to the man and say, 'It's a mannequin with its head chopped off. I use that exact model to display the clothes in the women's section of my department stores.' But this was a networking night. He hadn't paid forty thousand dollars for his and Claudia's tickets to get into an argument with a man who might one day be useful to him. You didn't get to the top of your game by being rude and alienating people. New York was a big city, but paths crossed in unexpected places and by unexpected means. Besides, the man didn't mean any harm. Chances were he was scouting for opinions on the pieces so he could form his own opinions off the basis of them.

'Please excuse us,' Ciro said with a smile, 'but we still need to visit the Rodrigo room before the meal starts.' Whisking Claudia away, he said under his breath, 'Shall we go upstairs?'

'Definitely. I think I might die if I have to listen to any more.' Their eyes met again, amusement dancing between them, locking them together as co-conspirators. They were still laughing when they reached the second floor, which had been cleared of all 'art' to create a huge restaurant and dance floor. A rock band, famous for its hedonistic excesses, was tuning up on the stage, the drummer swigging from a bottle of vodka. As the evening went on, Ciro noticed the singer giving Claudia the eye. Lots of men were. He didn't blame them. Dressed in a long sparkling gold dress with spaghetti straps and which dipped in a V to skim over her growing cleavage, her glorious hair worn loose and falling like waves, she looked spellbindingly beautiful.

But it was more than her beauty that made him feel like the cat who'd got the cream. The shy woman who'd clung to his hand throughout their wedding celebrations and hung back to let him do all the talking had grown in confidence enough to instigate conversations and not just be carried along by them. A number of people at the gala had attended their wedding and, though he knew it shouldn't surprise him, he was still surprised when she remembered their names without having to be prompted. What a memory she had. What a woman she was.

Later, as he held her tightly on the dance floor, it suddenly came to him that he no longer saw her father whenever he looked at her. All he saw was Claudia, his beautiful, brave wife...

His heart made a sudden lunge as his head sped forwards six months. To when she would leave.

CHAPTER THIRTEEN

As Ciro had a week-long trip to Japan starting the next day, he insisted on taking Claudia out for dinner on Sunday evening. The restaurant he chose was a small, exclusive place famed, according to Ciro, for its excellent cuisine. It was only a short walk from the apartment, and they strolled the busy streets to it with their hands clasped together. For the first time since her arrival in New York, Claudia felt comfortable walking through it. She doubted she would ever think herself a native New Yorker but it was good not to feel like a complete alien in her new home city. She was certain that when the time came to move into her own apartment, she'd be able to embrace the freedom without fear.

'I've had an idea for a career,' she said when they'd finished the first of their nine-course tasting menu.

His eyes sparked with lively interest. 'Tell me.'

'I thought I could open a cake business.'

He grinned. 'Excellent idea. Marcy keeps raving about the cake you made for her daughter.'

'She's asked me to make her a Christmas cake and her sister's asked me to make a cake for her wedding anniversary,' she told him, unable to contain her pride. 'Her cousin's getting married next year and wants me to make the cake for that too. And they want to pay me for them!'

'So they should. Do you want to open a shop?'

'Gosh, no!' She shuddered. Then she thought again. 'Maybe one day,' she pondered, thinking aloud. 'When the baby's older and not dependent on me as much. But for the time being I thought I'd go with word of mouth. I thought I could ask for testimonials from them and take lots of pictures to build up a portfolio, then when I'm ready and our baby's older and I'm hopefully...' she held up crossed fingers '...able to read more, I can get a professional website done. When it gets to that stage, could I speak to someone from your marketing team for advice?'

'Of course. I said I'd give you whatever help you need. I meant it.'

'Thank you.' She sighed.

'What's wrong?'

She shrugged. 'It's just so frustrating that even now, when I have the chance to make something of myself, I still need help. It's frustrating to know I'll always need help.'

'There's nothing wrong with asking for help when you need it. I would never have created my own business if I hadn't asked.'

'Did you?'

He nodded. 'My first store was a derelict building six blocks from here. I saw its potential but I didn't have the cash to buy it or do any of the things needed to remodel it or buy stock in or anything.'

The waiter arrived back at the table with their second course, which to Claudia's eyes looked like a giant langoustine artfully draped with skinny brown sticks in a white broth with a bit of lettuce on the side, and which took longer to describe than it must have taken the chef to cook.

When she took her first bite though, her taste buds exploded and she made a mental note to beg the chef for the recipe.

'How did you get the money?' Claudia asked when they'd finished the dish, keen to hear more. 'Did you go to the bank?'

'Three banks turned me down. Then I remembered my friend Ollie's father was a private investor so I asked him for the loan.'

'And he gave it to you?'

'Yes. I sold the store two years later—I came to dislike the location—and paid the whole loan back plus interest, and I had enough left over to get a mortgage on the building that became my flagship store. The rest is history. If I hadn't asked for that loan you and I wouldn't be sitting here.'

'What would you have done?'

'I don't know. I knew I wanted to see the world and make a fortune. I knew I had a good business brain and an analytical mind. I had the potential and knew I would recognise the opportunity when it came along. And now I have lots of business interests.'

'Other than the department stores?'

'I invest in graduates like myself. If they have a business idea I can see working, then I invest in them. If you decide you want to open your own shop, I expect you to give me first refusal as backer for it.'

'Only if it was a proper loan,' she said. 'I wouldn't want to be a charity case.'

'You're the mother of my child. You'll never be a charity case to me.'

Their third course was brought to the table. Claudia hadn't noticed them take the dishes from the second.

Once she'd swallowed the first delicious bite, she said, 'Can we look for an apartment for me after Christmas?'

Green eyes found hers and held the stare before he had a drink of his wine. 'That soon?'

'We did say we'd look in the new year,' she

pointed out. 'New York doesn't frighten me any more. I'm learning my way around and becoming comfortable with it. I feel ready to make the move now. I'm not bothered about the location, although somewhere close to you would be great, and I'm not bothered about the size. All I'll need are two bedrooms but if I'm going to make a success of the cake business, I'll need a decent-sized kitchen.' She pulled a rueful face. 'I struggled for space when I made the birthday cake.'

'Don't you like my kitchen?' he teased, although there was something in his eyes that bothered her.

She tried to be diplomatic. 'It's pretty basic.'

'Basic?' He arched a brow.

She smiled. 'In proportion to the rest of the apartment it's tiny. And its layout's impractical if you're trying to make more than one thing at a time.'

'I thought you liked my apartment?'

'I love it. I just hate the kitchen.' Remembering that he'd remodelled the entire apartment to his specific tastes, she felt herself blush. 'Sorry.'

It had been many weeks since Ciro had seen such a dark stain of colour cover her cheeks.

'Don't be sorry. The kitchen was an afterthought to everything else I had done. It was rarely used before you moved in.'

'You surprise me,' she said drily.

He grinned. 'But if you hate it so much, I can get an architect friend of mine to look at reconfiguring things. The staffroom's never used. We can knock into it and create a space that's twice what we currently have for you.'

Confusion flittered in her eyes. 'Why would you do that?'

He leaned across the table to take hold of her hand. He'd spent the day waiting for the right moment to broach this. That time was now. 'Because, *bedda*, I want you to stay.

Her eyes flickered.

'I want you to stay. When the baby comes. Stay with me. Be a family.'

Now her eyes drifted down to their clasped hands. Slowly, she extracted hers and rested them both on her lap. 'This is rather sudden.'

'I've been thinking about it for weeks.' Since the dream he'd had of their baby and the knowledge that he could love it—that a part of him already did love it—Ciro had thought of little else. The strong feelings he'd experienced at the gala had only cemented what he already knew. 'I don't see the point in you moving into your own place any more, not now that things have changed so much between us. You and me... we're great together. Our child will have two parents under one roof and you won't have to navigate the world alone. I'll be there to support you in everything you do.'

It felt as if an age passed while he waited for her to respond. 'I had no idea you were thinking along those lines.'

'You must see it makes perfect sense.'

She shook her head and reached for her water.

'I understand your caution,' he admitted.

Her expression was wary. 'Do you?'

He drained his wine and stared at her intently. 'I've treated you terribly. I blamed you for your father's actions. I've been cruel. Horrible. My only excuse is that I've been grieving for my father.' He closed his eyes and sucked in a breath to counter the torturous throb thinking of his father always produced. 'His death is the single biggest pain I've felt in my life. I felt such guilt. I *feel* such guilt. I should have visited more. I should have picked up the phone more. I should have made myself more available. I made the fatal assumption of thinking he would always be there for me. Do you remember how you told me you can't change the past? Well, that's what I've been struggling with, because I want to change it. I want to turn back time and be there for him and shoulder that burden. I want to be there for my *mamma* too.'

Claudia's head remained bowed but he knew she was listening to every word.

He leaned forward. 'I need to slow down. I've been so busy setting the world on fire over the last decade that I never stopped long enough to meet someone I could share my life with. Marriage was always something for the future. Now I have you and a baby on the way, I feel differently. I'm ready to be a father. The times we've spent living together, getting to know each other… I don't deny that I got you wrong. Badly wrong. But I swear that's all in the past. We can look to the future, starting now. We can remodel the kitchen to make it more practical for you— hell, we can buy a house with a garden if that's what you want. Just tell me what you need and I will make it happen.'

It seemed to take for ever for her eyes to meet his. Sadness shone from them. 'I'm sorry, Ciro, but this isn't what I want. Maybe it will be one day, but not yet. And I don't think you want it either.'

'Haven't I just told you that it *is* what I want? And I *know* you want it too.' Heat pulsed through him to think of how she came apart in his arms and the intensity of what they shared. The future he'd spent the day imagining for them blazed in bright, sunny colours.

A sudden spark of anger blew the sadness away from her eyes. 'Stop making assumptions,' she said tightly. 'You always do that. You assumed I was like my father and now that you've decided I'm nothing like him you assume, because it's nice and convenient for you, that what I really want is to give up the freedom I've spent my entire life waiting for to continue a marriage that was only ever a lie.'

His belief that she'd be enthusiastic about his plans for their future dissolved. Coldness crept into his bloodstream. 'I've apologised for that numerous times.'

'I know, and I do believe you're sincere, but what you did forced me to think properly about my life and the kind of future I want. We both knew when I moved in with you that it would only be temporary. Us becoming lovers has changed things but it hasn't changed my plans and I haven't said *anything* to make you believe differently.'

'What happens to us, then?' he challenged. 'I buy you an apartment, you leave and that's it, we're over?'

Her brows drew together. 'Why would it be over? We can still be together. I don't have to move far. We can still be a family, just not in the traditional sense. Maybe it will happen one day but not yet. I'm not ready for that.'

The coldness in his blood rose to form an icy pounding in his head. 'Not ready for it? It's the life we're already living.'

'But it was only ever temporary.' Closing her eyes, she put her elbow on the table and rested her forehead in her hand. 'I want my freedom. That's all I've ever wanted, the freedom to get out of bed knowing I'm not answerable to anyone, the freedom to make my own choices…the freedom to just be *me*.'

His guts coiling and knotting, Ciro waved to a passing waiter for a fresh drink. Then he fixed his attention back on Claudia and drummed his fingers on the table. 'You know, *bedda*, in all the time we've been together, I've not said anything about the fact you used me or asked you to apologise for it.'

She visibly recoiled. 'I have *never* used you.'

'I was your escape plan from your father.'

'That's not all you were. I was crazy about you.'

Her use of the past tense only made the tempest in his guts rage more violently. While he'd been basking in the headiness of their lovemaking and thinking of a future as a family for them, she'd been marking down the days until she could leave him.

'I was your escape plan and now I'm just your convenient bolt-hole and soon I'll be the convenient bank account to buy you a home of your own.'

Now her brows shot upwards. 'Don't make it

sound like I'm demanding you buy me an apartment. If you'd had your way, you'd have installed me in one the minute I arrived in New York! And it's not for *my* convenience. It's so our baby can grow up with both its parents in the same city.'

'Sure you don't want me to have custody?' he retorted scathingly. 'I'd have thought having a baby will cramp your style when you finally get the freedom you want so badly.'

Her face drained of colour. 'That's unfair,' she whispered. 'I love our baby, you know that, and I will do whatever it takes to give it the best start in life. He or she's the reason I'm here and you know that too. Whatever freedoms I have to give up for it will be no sacrifice at all.'

'But it would be a sacrifice to give up those so-called freedoms for me?'

'That's completely different and you know it. You don't want me to give up my future because you're in love with me but because you've decided that as I'm here and not as bad as you thought, then I'll do.'

The waiter arrived with another bottle of wine. He poured Ciro a glass. Ciro downed it in one then, his face a grimacing mask, got to his feet and pulled his wallet out of his back pocket.

'What are you doing?' Claudia asked, trying to make sense of how a conversation that had started with support and laughter had descended into such poison and so quickly.

Live with Ciro permanently? He hadn't given even a hint he'd been thinking about it. And now that *she* was thinking it, all she felt was a familiar fear.

'Going home. I've lost my appetite.' He pulled out a wedge of bills without counting them and threw them on the table. 'Are you coming? Or shall I call a cab for you?'

'I'll come with you.' But she'd barely finished speaking when he strode to the exit.

Shrugging her jacket on, she hurried to catch up to him and was relieved to find him waiting on the street for her, his face the same mask.

They didn't exchange a single word on the walk back to the apartment. Ciro kept his hands rammed in his jacket pocket and his chin jutted out. But he kept his strides to a length that made it manageable for her to keep pace, a gesture that made both her heart ache and anger froth.

Why did he have to spring this on her like that? They'd discussed her future plans many times. He'd given her every encouragement in them, and now he was acting as if she were the unreasonable one for not falling into line just because he'd changed his mind.

He wasn't even asking her to stay for her!

When they stepped into the apartment,

he didn't pause to remove his shoes, heading straight up the stairs, climbing them two at a time.

She found him in the bedroom, his suit already stripped from his magnificent body.

The look of contempt he threw her as he strode into the bathroom made her veins freeze.

She shook her head, trying to clear the white noise filling it. 'This is ridiculous.'

He opened the bathroom cabinet. 'Wanting to be a proper family with my wife and child is ridiculous, is it?'

'No, but getting angry with me because I don't want to live with you is. I rushed into marriage with you before without opening my eyes and I won't commit my future and throw away my freedom to you again until I'm certain we can make it work, and I won't have you bullying me into making a snap decision on something I might live to regret again on a whim.'

'*Bullying* you?' he snarled, slamming the cabinet door shut without having removed anything from it. 'You sleep with me every night. You act as if you care for me…'

'I *do* care for you. Very much.'

'But not enough to give up your precious freedom.'

'Not when my freedom's come at such a high price.' Her whole body trembled. 'My entire life has been built on lies. The father I love is a monster. My childhood was one massive lie. The man I thought I loved lied in God's house when we made our wedding vows. I've been lied to over and over again, and all to keep me under the thumb and in the power of men. Can you blame me for wanting my freedom? Can you blame me for being cautious?'

The pulse on his temple throbbed madly. 'You're comparing me with your father?'

'You've just done that all by yourself.'

Cold green eyes bore into hers for endless seconds before a flame of anger shot through them and he left the bathroom and strode into his dressing room.

He left the door open and swiftly pulled a pair of jeans on. 'I'm going to check into a hotel.'

She gritted her teeth. 'Why?'

Stretching a T-shirt over his head, he tugged it over his broad chest then strolled back into the room and over to Claudia's favourite nude painting and pulled it off the wall. To her disbelief, she saw that it hid a safe. If she didn't feel as if she'd just had a truck slam into her stomach she would laugh at the cliché.

Moments later a green light flashed and the safe door swung open. From it Ciro pulled out a battered briefcase, which he opened with a stony-faced flourish. It contained money. A lot of money.

'Here's five million dollars,' he said in the same monotone. 'Take it. It's yours. Marcy will be at her desk early. Give her your bank account details and I'll transfer another five million. That along with this apartment should be sufficient payment for a marriage that's only lasted three months.'

'You're *ending* things?' Her brain felt numb but her heart and everything else inside her contracted and throbbed violently.

'How can I end something that was only temporary?' he shot back.

It was only as he walked towards the bedroom door that she realised he really did mean to leave.

A shot of furious adrenaline pulsed through her veins and she darted past him to block his exit. 'What is wrong with you?'

'I'll tell you what's wrong, *Princess*. Thinking we could have a future together. Thinking we could be a family. I've done everything in my power to make up for the wrongs I did to you, but it isn't enough. You won't trust me. You won't even consider making things permanent between us because you've got it in your head that the minute you agree I'm going to lock a ball and chain on you and stamp my thumbprint on your forehead—*just like your father*. That you can think such things of me…' His nostrils flared with disdain. 'You want your freedom? Well, guess what, Princess? Your freedom starts now. I'll sign the apartment over to you. *Fitting*, don't you think?'

'I don't want your apartment,' she cried. Feeling herself on the verge of swearing, something she never did, she sucked in a breath.

'It's the safest place for my child,' he responded coldly. His arms wrapped around his chest, the muscles in his biceps bulging. 'It has security and people on hand if you need them.' A burst of emotion flared in his voice. 'Don't think for a second that I will abdicate my responsibility for her. I love our baby and I *will* be a father to her. Try and keep her from me and I will fight you. Now move or I will move you.'

He would do it. Everything on his face and in his body language told her he would scoop her up and set her aside if she didn't let him pass.

Folding her arms tightly across her chest, Claudia raised herself onto her toes so her face was as close to his as it could be without having to touch him. She was barely aware of the tears falling down her cheeks until she opened her mouth and tasted their saltiness. 'You wonder why I can't trust you when you treat me like this? When you throw me to one side because I won't roll over and abide by your wishes? I've had a lifetime of being a doormat. If I'm going to have a real marriage then I want one that's got love at its core and which is built on mutual respect. If you'd shown a little more patience maybe I would have found that with you but you don't *have* any patience; everything has to be immediate. You didn't give yourself time to grieve for your father because you were too consumed with your vengeance and now you're eaten with guilt and think a ready-made family will ease it.'

'Don't you *dare* bring my father into this.' His eyes had become blocks of emerald ice.

'He's the reason we're here!' Claudia's chin trembled so hard and her throat was so constricted that getting the words out hurt. 'I forgave you a long time ago for your despicable lies because I understood you were acting out of grief for him. I *made* myself forgive you for our baby's sake. I hope for our baby's sake that one day you can forgive yourself too.'

His expression didn't change. She might as well have been talking to a brick wall.

His expression didn't alter either when he clamped his hands on her sides, lifted her off her feet and moved her two steps away from the door.

He didn't look back as he walked down the stairs and out of the apartment and out of her life.

CHAPTER FOURTEEN

THE BUSTLE, BRIGHT colours and noise of Tokyo were something Ciro normally enjoyed. He'd only been to the city a couple of times before and found it an energising and fascinating place to be. Like when he worked in the Middle East, the business practices and customs were different from what he was used to, something he usually relished. On this trip he couldn't find any enthusiasm for anything, not even the huge building he was in the process of buying.

When he'd thought his future involved a family he'd considered making this the last purchase of his business empire.

As he gazed out of his hotel window, far too wired to sleep even though it was two a.m. Tokyo time, a message came through from his lawyer. The cash offer he'd made for an apartment three blocks from his department store had been accepted. Once the cash was transferred, it would be his. He fired a message back telling him to get the deal finalised immediately, then messaged Marcy with instructions to get the new apartment furnished. Ciro disliked staying in hotels. Even the most opulent of them were bland and generic to his eyes. If he could return to Manhattan and have the new apartment ready for him to move into, that would be one less aggravation.

No sooner had he pressed send on the message than his phone vibrated in his hand.

A cold sweat broke out on his forehead when he saw the name of the caller. It was Claudia.

He hadn't seen or spoken to her since he'd walked out four days ago. He'd tried hard not to think about her too. It had proved impossible.

Suddenly wishing he had a strong drink in hand, he took a deep breath and answered it. 'Yes?'

The gentle sound of her clearing her throat echoed into his ear. 'Ciro?'

'Yes. Is everything okay?'

'I've just had a call from the clinic.'

His heart rate, already erratic from the sound of her voice, clattered violently. 'Is something wrong with the baby?'

'No, no, please don't worry. They called to tell me I'd missed the scan appointment. I'm really sorry. They sent me a letter but they addressed it to Mrs Trapani and I didn't recognise the words so I didn't open it. I assumed it was for you and you'd open it when you got back from Japan. I've got a pile of letters waiting for you.'

'Give them to Marcy. What's happening with the scan? Are they rearranging the appointment?'

'They can fit me in this afternoon. I said I'd speak to you—'

'You should go.'

'Are you sure? I don't want you to miss it.' Her anxiety at this made his clattering heart give a sudden wrench. 'We can rearrange it for when you get back.'

'No. Go ahead. Scans are important. We can book another one further down the line that I'll come along to. Take Marcy with you—she can deal with the paperwork.'

'I feel terrible. I'm so sorry.'

'Don't be. It isn't your fault.' The only person at fault was, as always, her bastard father. If he'd given her the help she'd needed all those years ago, Claudia wouldn't be so reliant on other people to do her reading for her. 'Let me know how it goes. And send me a video or a picture, okay?'

'Of course I will.'

'And, Claudia…?'

'Yes?'

'Thanks for letting me know.'

Her, 'You're welcome,' was a whisper that barely brushed his ears before the line went dead.

She'd hung up on him.

* * *

Claudia sat on the bed gazing at the framed scan of her baby daughter with a heart so full of love it choked her. She'd got Marcy to email Ciro the same picture and the video the clinic had made of it too. It warmed her cold bones to know he would be looking at it with the same love.

Her phone rang. Her heart caught and she held her breath as she pulled it out of her pocket. Would it be Ciro responding to the emails? Marcy had warned her he had back-to-back meetings that day. All the same, her stomach plummeted when she recognised her sister's name on the screen.

Looking at her reflection in the bedroom mirror, Claudia forced a smile to her face before answering the call. She'd seen a heroine do the same thing on a television show once, the smile supposedly inflecting in the voice. She had no idea why she felt the need to do it too or why she felt so flat, so…bereft.

She guessed that particular heroine didn't have a sister who could read voices. Imma listened to her greeting and her concern was immediate.

'I'm fine, I promise,' Claudia assured her. Imma already knew that she and Ciro had gone their separate ways. For once, Claudia hadn't confided everything, simply said they'd brought their day of parting forward. Too many bitter, hateful words had been exchanged for her to want to relive them.

'You've never been alone before,' Imma pointed out.

'I was alone whenever Ciro travelled on business. This is the same. Just longer.' Just permanent.

'Come back to Sicily,' Imma begged. 'Please. I'll look after you and the baby.'

'I don't need looking after,' she told her honestly. 'New York's my home now. I'm getting to know my way around, and Ciro's here if I need him.'

Imma snorted.

'He's my baby's father and he loves her,' Claudia said quietly. Ciro's vehemence in stating he would fight her if she tried to keep their baby from him had been heartfelt. She supposed such a threat should frighten her, but it didn't. She'd been terrified from the moment she'd taken the pregnancy test that he wouldn't be able to love their baby and now that she knew he did, she could sleep easier. Not that she'd been able to sleep much since they'd parted. It didn't matter how much she tried adjusting the air conditioning, her bones always felt too cold to sleep.

Maybe she just needed to get used to sleeping in the guest room. She hadn't been able to bring herself to sleep in the bed they'd shared.

They chatted a little longer, Imma filling her

in on everything going on back home in Sicily. At some point Claudia was going to have to return and visit her father. She spoke to him occasionally and though it broke her heart to avoid him, it was nothing less than he deserved. But he was still her father and she still loved him.

For what he'd done to Ciro's family and all the other families he'd hurt, though, she would never forgive him.

Ciro threw half the bagel he'd bought for his breakfast in the bin. He didn't know why but he found them bland now. He wondered if he'd damaged his taste buds because in recent weeks all food seemed bland to him.

As this was his first day off in a fortnight he set out to do what he'd promised himself he would do weeks ago and headed to the guest room that adjoined his new master suite. It would make an excellent nursery for the baby. That was if he stayed here long enough before the birth without selling up and buying somewhere else. As with his marriage, purchasing an apartment chosen and paid for in haste while on a trip to Japan meant he could repent at his leisure. When it came to this apartment, he had plenty of repenting to do. He hated the place.

When it came to his marriage…

He shoved the thought from his mind, just as

he always did when the image of Claudia floated in his head.

They spoke. They communicated, sometimes directly, sometimes through Marcy. But never in person. She had an obstetrician appointment next week that she'd invited him to attend. It would be the first time they'd seen each other since their parting.

How much easier it would be to hold onto his fury if she weren't so damn considerate. Typical Claudia, putting their baby first.

The only person she wouldn't put first, he thought grimly, was him.

Trying again to shove thoughts of Claudia aside, Ciro rubbed his hand over his mouth and contemplated the room's dimensions, pondering where best to place the nursery furniture, and then pondering what nursery furniture even entailed. There was a lot he had to learn before his daughter's birth.

His brain moving on to colour schemes, he opened the dressing-room door to double check it would be large enough for all the baby clothing he intended to buy. A couple of large cardboard boxes were neatly stacked in it.

He groaned. He'd got his staff to pack all his personal possessions for him at the old apartment—now Claudia's apartment—then unpack everything for him here at the new one.

Tempting though it was to leave the boxes and get his staff to sort them tomorrow, now he knew they were there, he figured he might as well just deal with them himself.

Crouching down before them, he picked at the packing tape of the top one then ripped it off.

Tissue paper covered the contents and he roughly pulled it out.

And then his heart stopped when he recognised the white Sicilian lace the tissue paper had been hiding.

Claudia's wedding dress.

Seeing that dress was like looking at a ghost.

He stared at it with blood rushing through his ears. The room began to spin.

Groping as if in a dream, he pulled the dress from the box and, getting to his feet, removed the clear plastic protector. Memories flooded him before he could stop them, filling him until every cell in his body throbbed. How beautiful she'd looked in this dress. How sincere her vows had been. How the last time he'd seen this dress had been when she'd point-blank refused to have the guest room and insisted on sharing his room with him.

He'd bought himself a new apartment but it was as if she'd come with him in spirit. She was everywhere he went. He couldn't go into the kitchen without seeing her there baking. He couldn't go into his new library without seeing her stretched out on his old reading sofa. He couldn't even use the bathroom without remembering the cute way she brushed her teeth.

And now this dress lay in his arms like a physical manifestation of her absence and the *pain* that tore through him…

The room spun harder and without any warning his legs gave way beneath him and he slumped to the floor.

Crumpling the dress to his chest, he held it tightly and tried to breathe. There was a stabbing burn behind his eyes that made the room become a blur. But he could still see her face. It was right there in his retinas. Her dazzling smile. Her sweetness. Her *goodness*. All radiating there in front of him, blazing with her fieriness. Her protectiveness. Her strength. Her bravery. This was a woman who'd grown up with only a pair of red shoes and an elusive scent to remember her mother by whereas he…

He'd had over thirty years with both his parents. His father was gone but he still had his mother. Claudia hadn't lost her father in a literal sense but in a figurative sense he was gone. The man she'd believed him to be didn't exist.

Ciro had grieved for his father and looked at the world through vengeful eyes, needing to strike back and *do* something to balm the pain in his heart. Claudia refused to be a victim. She did what she believed to be right in her heart and used her conscience to guide her. It would never occur to her to use their child as a weapon against him and she would be horrified if anyone suggested it.

And he'd walked away from her. And for what? Because she wasn't stupid enough to trust a man who'd betrayed her so badly with promises of for ever? Because the woman who'd been hidden away and suffocated all her life wanted to strike out and learn to breathe on her own?

He'd spouted about wanting to slow down but had expected Claudia to speed up and when she'd refused to move to his timescale, he'd dropped her like a hot stone, the insinuation he was like her father the last straw. She hadn't even said that—in his hurt and rage, he'd interpreted it like that because, as they said, the truth hurt. He *had* tried to browbeat her into falling in line with his plans. All he'd heard from her lips was rejection. His pride couldn't take it. As always with him, it had been all or nothing. No patience.

He'd never had any patience. Never had the ability to sit still for anything longer than a movie. Even the books he liked to read were fast-paced, the food he ate ordered for speed as much as taste.

Without him even noticing, Claudia had taught

him to slow down and enjoy the simple pleasures life had to offer.

She'd given up everything for their baby so Ciro could be a father to it. She'd fought tooth and nail for them to forge a relationship. And, as always, he'd wanted more. He always wanted more. He'd never been satisfied with his lot, always pushing, always striving for better, for greater.

Nothing in his life was or ever had been better or greater than Claudia.

Two days later and Ciro left the boardroom and headed to his office. The working day was almost done. As he passed his administration team, he noticed a group of them huddled around a desk. When they saw him, they parted like the Red Sea and scattered back to their desks.

He grimaced, not that they'd been talking together but that they were clearly wary of his mood. He'd be the first to admit he hadn't been the easiest person to work for in recent weeks.

And then he noticed what they'd all been huddled around. A box with the lid open revealed a two-tier cake decorated with an artistry and craftsmanship any *patissier* would be proud of. Instinct told him who this particular *patissier* was. Claudia's name, printed with a flourish on the side of the box, confirmed it. Marcy, with

Ciro's permission, had ordered the cake boxes for her.

'Is there a celebration I should know about?' he asked Rachel, the woman whose desk the cake was on.

She managed a quick, wary smile. 'It's my cousin's twenty-first birthday.'

He had no idea if his staff knew he'd left Claudia. Marcy was utterly discreet but his staff had eyes. He did not employ stupid people. He cleared his throat. 'I hope your cousin likes it. You're having a party?'

She nodded.

Reaching into his back pocket, he pulled his wallet out and removed two hundred dollars. He handed the cash to Rachel. 'Wish her a happy birthday and get the first drinks in on me.'

Her surprised words of thanks were distant echoes as he left her and continued to his office.

He locked the door and slumped into his chair, cradling his head as the latest wave of pain he'd been fighting since seeing that cake finally unleashed inside him.

Everything inside him hurt.

He couldn't describe even to himself how much pain he was in. But he welcomed it too. This was what he deserved: every ounce of pain as penance for what he'd done to the purest-hearted woman to walk the earth.

When the wave had subsided, he stared at the wall of his office that partitioned the lobby. On the other side of the lobby was the apartment. Claudia was in there. What was she doing? Baking another cake? Cooking something else? Listening to a book? Watching a movie?

He hadn't set eyes on her in three weeks.

They had been the most painful three weeks of his life. He had no idea how he was going to react when he saw her in a few days at the obstetrician appointment.

He had no idea if he could wait that long to see her again. He missed her more than he'd known it was humanly possible to miss someone.

Claudia turned the dishwasher on and, with a sigh, filled the sink for the items she didn't trust the dishwasher with. She picked up one of her new knives. The knife set was the first thing she'd bought with the money she'd been paid for a cake she'd made. It was the first money she'd ever earned and it had felt even more amazing than she'd dreamed.

But the joy of the moment had been tainted when she'd picked up her phone to share her joy with Ciro and had put it down without calling him. He wouldn't want to hear it.

She'd called Imma instead but it hadn't been the same. It was Ciro she'd wanted to share the moment with. It was Ciro she'd longed to show the cake boxes with her name emblazoned on them.

Because it was Ciro who'd never let her illiteracy define her or allowed *her* to let it define her.

Closing her eyes, she sent a prayer for the pain in her heart to ease some time soon. *And, please, God, let me stop missing him. It hurts too much.*

Only three more days and she would see him again. The pregnancy was accelerating. Soon she would be overwhelmed with appointments for baby checks. Through the messages they'd exchanged, she knew Ciro would want to attend all of them.

Putting the sharp knife into the hot, soapy water, she knew she had to get a handle on her emotions, and soon. She had to stay strong like Elizabeth Bennet. Even when Elizabeth realised Mr Darcy wasn't the unpleasant, arrogant man she'd believed him to be and her feelings developed into a love she didn't think could be realised, she remained strong...

Love?

There was a lurch in Claudia's stomach so strong that she reflexively tightened her fingers around the sharp blade of the knife.

The water in the sink quickly turned red. She gazed at it in horror and lifted her shaking hand out, feeling as if she'd slipped into a nightmare.

All four fingers of her left hand had a slice mark where they joined her hand. All four slices were dripping blood. Red splatters hit the floor.

She couldn't get her brain to unfreeze enough to tend to the wounds. Horror thrashed through her veins and into her heart. Her breaths became shallow. She couldn't take in air. The room began to move, not in a full-powered spin but in stomach-churning slow motion.

She loved Ciro.

Her stomach tightened. She blinked and put her good hand to it and felt it tighten again. That was her baby.

She could feel her baby!

Finally getting air into her lungs, she took a clean tea towel out of the drawer and absently wound it over her wounded fingers, all the while her brain racing at a hundred miles an hour. She needed to share this moment with Ciro. He would want to know.

He should be here sharing it with her…

The wail rose up her throat and escaped from her mouth before she even knew it had formed.

The slow-motion spinning accelerated and she grabbed hold of the worktop to stop herself falling. She could do nothing to stop the tears falling. She could do nothing to stop the sobs ripping out of her.

It took for ever before she had herself under

any semblance of control but the feeling of being in a dream/nightmare didn't lessen and it was with her feet working of their own accord that she headed for the front door, wiping fresh tears from her eyes every other step.

She needed to find Ciro. He needed to know she'd felt their baby move. He was still in the building. She knew it in her heart. All she had to do was find him.

She opened the front door and for a split second thought she really had fallen into a dream.

Standing on the other side of it, his finger poised to ring the intercom, stood Ciro.

CHAPTER FIFTEEN

ALL THE AIR was punched out of Ciro at the first sight of her. He could barely remember walking from his office to the apartment. Once minute he'd been at his desk, the next his legs had been moving, the only thing with any solidity the image of Claudia that had become stuck on his vision.

And there she stood, right before him, her face blotchy, half of her plaited hair undone, eyes red…

'What's wrong?' he asked, snapping from stupor to alert in an instant. And then he noticed the tea towel wrapped around her hand and the blood soaking through it. 'My God, you're hurt.'

She shook her head but the tears spilling down her face told him a very different story.

'We need to get you to hospital.'

But her head shook again and her throat moved a number of times before she croaked, 'It looks worse than it is.'

Working on automatic pilot, he put an arm around her waist and gently led her back inside. He had to fight through the loud pulse in his ears to think coherently. There was a first-aid kit in the kitchen. He would look at her injury there. If he judged it to be serious he would take her straight to hospital, whether she wanted him to or not.

She let him guide her, as meek as a newborn lamb.

The sight he found in the kitchen only increased his horror. It was as if a massacre had taken place. There was blood on the hardwood floor, on the kitchen counter, in the sink...

Sitting her on the window seat, he hurried to the cupboard with the kit in it and grabbed it, then was back at her side in a flash.

Not a word was exchanged as she let him carefully unpeel the tea towel.

He winced to see the damage and quickly pressed the tea towel back into place, ordering her to hold it tight. She complied.

'This needs medical attention,' he said as he ripped through the wrapping of a fresh, sterile bandage. 'We need to get you to hospital. No arguing. I'll call my driver. He'll get the car ready for us.'

'No! It isn't that bad. Really.'

'For my own peace of mind, will you please let me take you there?'

'It'll be a waste of time and money.'

'*Bedda*, it looks like a slaughterhouse in here.'

She winced. 'It only looks that bad because I had a mad few moments and didn't do anything to stop the bleeding.'

'Why wouldn't you tend to something like this immediately?' he asked, bewildered at this kind of irrationality from someone usually so level-headed.

'I…' She swallowed and clamped her lips back together.

'Look, I'm going to call my doctor out, okay? I won't be able to rest until you've had a professional look at the wounds.' Not waiting for her to answer, he made the call.

When he ended the call, he found her looking at him, her dark brown eyes glistening.

'I felt the baby move.'

'Did you?' His heart thumped. 'What did it feel like?'

'Magical.' A tear fell down her cheek. 'I'm sorry you weren't there to share it. That's where I was going. To find you. So I could tell you.'

'You put off doing anything about your hand because you wanted to tell me the baby moved?'

'It didn't hurt much,' she mumbled, looking away. But then her gaze shot back to him and something like focus came into her eyes. 'What were you doing at the door? Were you coming to see me?'

He took a deep inhalation and nodded.

'Why?'

The heavy weight compressing his chest spread to smother his throat. It took a moment for him to clear it.

Tentatively, he took her uninjured hand in his. The weight loosened a fraction when she didn't immediately tug it away. The beautiful brown eyes that rarely missed anything kept a steadfast gaze on him.

'I just...' he cleared his throat again '...needed to see you. *Bedda*... I've missed you.'

She drew a sharp breath.

He brought her hand to his lips and pressed a kiss to it. 'I'm sorry, *bedda*. For how I reacted. For running away. For being an arrogant, impatient bastard.'

Her throat moved as she breathed deeply through her pretty, snub nose.

His heart ached to look at her. Everything in him ached.

He'd hurt her so much and in so many ways. How could she bear to share the same air as him?

'I've always been impatient,' he said. 'I had so many dreams as a little boy and I couldn't wait to get out into the world and live them. I was always pushing, always striving for the next fix, always restless. I neglected my parents. Not deliberately but I took them for granted. I fitted them into *my* schedule, never considering how they would drop everything for one of my visits. I knew they were proud of me and that felt great. Because it was all about *me*. When my father died…' He breathed into her hand. The softness of her skin soothed his raging heartbeats. The gentleness of her stare felt as if his soul were being bathed in honey.

'You know how much his death devastated me,' he said quietly. 'You were right about so many things. I *didn't* give myself time to grieve. And I did blame myself as much as I blamed your father. I don't know if Papà thought of confiding his troubles in me. I don't know because I wasn't there. When I left Sicily at eighteen, I left body and soul and my parents knew it. That is something else I must live with—my neglect of the two people who gave me more love than a child could wish for. But you were wrong about one thing.'

Her eyes flickered.

'I don't want a ready-made family with you to ease my guilt or because it's convenient.'

He let go of her hand and dragged his fingers down his face. The sigh he gave contained such hopelessness that Claudia's heart wrenched to hear it.

'You made me feel things right from the start. Real feelings. And then I found myself trapped in a hell of my own making, locked in a marriage with my enemy's daughter and I couldn't handle it. Even when I asked you to stay and be a family, I was fighting the truth.'

'Which is?' she whispered.

'That I love you. These weeks without you have been the worst of my life. I am broken without you. You, Claudia Buscetta—and you must always wear your name with pride because your goodness counteracts every one of your father's evil deeds—are the most loving, beautiful human being in the world. You deserve so much more than life has given you and I will regret my treatment of you to my dying day. I am here to ask—beg—you to give me one more chance. Please. I can't breathe without you. I'll accept whatever terms you make but, please, I beg you, let me share your life as well as our baby's life.'

As Claudia listened to this most prideful of men bear his soul, the last of the coldness that had enveloped her since he'd left melted away and sunshine heated her skin.

Leaning closer to him, she palmed his cheek. Now that she dared look at him properly, she saw the weight of the grief lining his handsome features. His eyes were heavy with sleep deprivation. He needed a shave.

'You never asked how I injured myself,' she said quietly.

His pain-filled eyes flashed with curiosity.

She rubbed her nose to his. Her senses exploded with joy as his woody scent hit her. 'I accidentally cut myself because I suddenly realised I love you. A moment later our baby moved. Ciro, it felt like she was kicking sense into me.'

He stared at her, brow furrowed with confusion.

'You're not the only one who's been fighting their feelings.' She stroked his cheekbone. 'I was too frightened to trust you again and *terrified* of trusting my feelings for you. I kept going over the past rather than thinking of all the wonderful things you've done for me in the present. You refused to let me make excuses for myself. You forced me to stand tall and be counted. *That's* what you've given me, Ciro, my self-respect. If having the freedom to live without you means being cold to my bones for the rest of my life then it's a freedom I don't want. The only freedom I want is the freedom to love you and wake beside you every day and the freedom to know you will love and support me in everything I do, just as I will love and support you in everything you do.'

Ciro's heart thudded. He hardly dared believe what Claudia's mouth and loving eyes were saying. He swallowed. 'You love me?'

'Yes. I love you,' she repeated softly against his lips. 'And I want to spend the rest of my life with you. Together. Under the same roof. You, me and our daughter. You're my world, Ciro.'

Something cracked deep inside him, a fissure that ripped open, expelling the last of the darkness that had made itself at home in him since his father's death. Into its place poured dazzling sunlight. Wrapping his arms around her, he crushed his mouth to hers and kissed her with all the love flowing in his heart.

'Oh, my beautiful love,' he whispered. 'I swear I will always love and cherish you. Always.'

'Always,' she echoed.

And he did love and cherish her. Always.

EPILOGUE

CIRO DROVE THROUGH the security gates that protected this exclusive New York suburb, nodded at the two guards on duty, and continued to the end of the long drive where he drove through another electric gate, this one exclusively protecting his estate. As happened every day of his working life, his heart lifted to see his huge white home gleaming under the sun and he had to resist putting his foot down to get there quicker. With three children, there was always the risk one of them might come flying out from behind one of the trees in the orchard to spray his car with rubber bullets.

He got out, threw his keys at his head groundsman to park for him and hurried into the house.

To his disappointment, Claudia wasn't in. The huge kitchen, with its three hobs and three ovens designed by her own beautiful hands, was filled with jars of jam she'd made from the fruit she grew in their huge plot. They would go into the

Christmas hampers she made every year for his Manhattan store, a natural follow-on from the cake-shop concession she'd opened in it and which had proved to be a massive hit with his clientele.

There were no labels on the jars. That would be done by the assistant Ciro employed for her. Suddenly hungry, he wondered if she'd notice if he opened one of them to spread over the crumpets she'd made the day before.

About to pilfer one of the jars, he suddenly noticed the letter left on the kitchen island, which by itself was as large as the kitchen of his old apartment.

Written in large, unsteady, childish writing, the note said:

Dear Ciro
Taken Alessandro and Roberto swimming.
Rosa at playdate.
I love you.
Claudia xxxxx

Seeing Claudia's penmanship never failed to choke him. He knew she would have perspired with the strain of writing this simple letter.

His beautiful, brave wife would never be able to read fluently—their youngest child, three-year-old Roberto, had an older reading age—

but every letter written and every letter read was a feat of endurance that filled him with more pride than he could contain.

He was about to swallow his first bite of crumpet when the front door flew open and his two youngest children hurled themselves at him like ballistic missiles. Their mother followed, took one look at what was in his hand and the opened jam jar on the counter, and her eyes narrowed.

Using their children as a human shield failed to save him from her. She wrapped her arms around his neck and licked the jam from the corner of his mouth. 'You, Ciro Trapani, are in so much trouble.'

'Are you going to punish me?' he murmured, squeezing her peachy bottom.

'Oh, yes,' she breathed.

'I can't wait.'

That night, baby number four was conceived.

* * * * *